Thomas Bland, James G. Cooper

Papers on North American Helicidæ

and on the geographical distribution of West India land shells

Thomas Bland, James G. Cooper

Papers on North American Helicidæ
and on the geographical distribution of West India land shells

ISBN/EAN: 9783337392499

Printed in Europe, USA, Canada, Australia, Japan

Cover: Foto ©Andreas Hilbeck / pixelio.de

More available books at **www.hansebooks.com**

PAPERS

ON

NORTH AMERICAN HELICIDÆ,

AND ON

THE GEOGRAPHICAL DISTRIBUTION OF WEST INDIA LAND SHELLS.

BY

THOMAS BLAND, F.G.S., LONDON,

MEMBER OF THE LYCEUM OF NATURAL HISTORY, NEW YORK; CORRESPONDING MEMBER OF THE
ACADEMY OF NATURAL SCIENCES, PHILADELPHIA, ETC.

ALSO

NOTICE OF LAND AND FRESHWATER SHELLS FROM THE ROCKY MOUNTAINS.

BY

T. BLAND AND DR. J. G. COOPER.

REPRINTED FROM THE ANNALS OF THE LYCEUM OF NATURAL HISTORY, NEW YORK.
VOLS. VI. AND VII.

NEW YORK:

BAILLIÈRE BROTHERS, 440 BROADWAY.

LONDON:—H. BAILLIÈRE, 219 REGENT STREET.

PARIS:—J. B. BAILLIÈRE ET FILS, RUE HAUTEFEUILLE.

MADRID:—C. BAILLY-BAILLIÈRE, CALLE DEL PRINCIPE.

1862.

CONTENTS.

Papers by Thomas Bland.

Paper by T. Bland and J. G. Cooper.

REMARKS

ON

CERTAIN SPECIES

OF

NORTH AMERICAN HELICIDÆ,

WITH

DESCRIPTIONS OF NEW SPECIES.

BY

THOMAS BLAND, F.G.S., LONDON,

MEMBER OF THE LYCEUM OF NATURAL HISTORY, NEW YORK; CORRESPONDING MEMBER OF THE
ACADEMY OF NATURAL SCIENCES, PHILADELPHIA, &c.

REPRINTED FROM THE ANNALS OF THE LYCEUM OF NATURAL HISTORY,
NEW YORK. VOL. VI.

PART I.

NEW YORK:

H. BAILLIÈRE, 290 BROADWAY.

LONDON:—H. BAILLIÈRE, 219 REGENT STREET.

PARIS:—J. B. BAILLIÈRE ET FILS, RUE HAUTEFEUILLE.

MADRID:—C. BAILLY-BAILLIÈRE, CALLE DEL PRINCIPE.

1858.

CONTENTS.

DESCRIPTIONS OF NEW SPECIES.

REMARKS ON THE FOLLOWING SPECIES, VIZ.:

DESCRIPTION

Two New Species of North American Helicidæ.

By Thos. Bland.

Reprinted from the Annals of the Lyceum of Natural History, February, 1858.

1.—Helix Edvardsi.

Plate IX. Fig. 14–16.

T. imperforatâ, lenticulari, carinatâ, tenuiusculâ, fulvâ; epidermide castaneâ, supra in striis pilosis prostratis minutis elevatâ,—infra tuber-culis acutis minutis creberrime munitâ, quæ juxta aperturam setos erectos gerunt; spirâ convexo-conoideâ; anfr. 5, complanatis, lente accrescentibus; ultimo antice gibbo, subito subdeflexo; apice minute granulato; basi convexo, parum indentatâ, lineis numerosis spiralibus sub epidermide impressis; suturâ profunde impressâ; aperturâ obliquâ, transversâ, auriformi; dente angustâ, subarcuatâ, lamelliformi, præ-longâ, parietis aperturalis coarctatâ; perist. margine supero acuto, parum reflexo, infero subarcuato, depresso, subreflexo, et ad anfractum ultimum subappresso, callo dentiformi intus instructo, obsolete inciso.

Shell imperforate, lenticular, carinate, the carina obsolete near the aperture, rather thin, beneath the epidermis pale brown ; the epidermis dark chestnut color, with numerous minute curved hair-like processes lying flat upon, and attached to the epidermidal surface of the upper whorls in the direction of the incremental striæ, the epidermis at the base covered with acute, raised, transverse tubercles, most numerous, and having erect bristles near the aperture ; spire convex-conoid ; whorls five, flattened, gradually increasing, the last gibbous above, suddenly but slightly deflected ; apex minutely granulate ; base convex, little indented in the umbilical region, and with impressed spiral lines beneath the epidermis ; suture deeply impressed ; aperture oblique, transverse, auriform, narrowed by a slender slightly arcuate lamelliform parietal tooth extending across from the umbilical axis, and terminating with a short angular deflection within the aperture ; upper margin of the peristome acute, scarcely reflected, lower margin slightly arcuate, depressed, slightly reflected, and partially appressed to the body whorl, with a tooth-like callus within, having an almost obsolete notch in the centre.

Diam. maj. 9, min. 8, alt. 5 mill.

Habitat.—Mountains in Fayette, or Green Briar Co., Virginia.   W. H. Edwards !

Observations.—This species is allied to or rather intermediate between *H. barbigera* Redf. (Plate IX. figs. 4–7), and *H. hirsuta* Say—the former connecting *H. spinosa* Lea with *H. fraterna* Say.   It is smaller, more elevated, less acutely carinated, and readily distinguished from *H. barbigera* by the partially appressed, notched peristome, and the different character of the epidermis.   In *H. barbigera* the attached hair-like epidermidal processes are produced, at the sutures and carina, into cilia which are entirely wanting in this species.   The same processes, though less numerous, and sometimes almost obso-

lete, are observable at the base of the former, while in the
latter, the basal epidermis approaches in character to that of
H. palliata Say. The deep characteristic notch in *H. hirsuta*
is considerably less developed in *H. Edcardsi*, and the callus
which connects the parietal tooth with the upper margin of
the peristome in the former, does not exist in the latter. In
the general character of the peristome the species under consideration resembles *H. hirsuta*, while *H. barbigera* is in that
particular more appropriately compared with *H. fraterna* Say.

While naming this species after my friend Mr. Edwards,
who collected it, I am quite aware of the objections to such
specific names, but in the Genus Helix it seems almost a hope-
less case to find, for a shell closely allied to several others, an
unpreoccupied name derived from any distinct specific character.

2.—Helix sculptilis.

Plate IX. Fig. 11–13.

T. obtecte perforatâ, suborbiculari, depressâ, subpellucidâ, pallide
corneâ, nitenti, lineis transversis regularibus concinne impressâ; spirâ
parum elevatâ, subconvexâ; anfr. 7, planulatis, ultimo rapide accres-
cente, prope aperturam ⅓ diam. subæquanti; basi planulatâ, leviter
excavatâ; suturâ parum impressâ; aperturâ subobliquâ, depressâ, transversâ, lunari; perist. simplici, acuto, sinuato, margine columellari
rapide et anguste reflexâ, et perforationem minutam tegenti.

Shell scarcely perforate, suborbicular, depressed, subpellucid,
pale horn color above, of lighter shade beneath, shining, with
regular, subequidistant, impressed transverse lines, those on
the last whorl extending over the periphery, and converging
in the umbilical excavation; spire very little elevated, scarcely
convex; whorls 7, planulate, the last rapidly increasing, equal
at the aperture to ⅓ the diam. of the shell, beneath flattened,
and little excavated in the umbilical region; suture lightly

impressed; aperture scarcely oblique, depressed, transverse, lunate; peristome simple, acute, sinuate, the columellar margin very rapidly and narrowly reflected over, and almost entirely covering the very small perforation.

Diam. maj. 12½, min. 11, alt. 5 mill.

Habitat.—"The Anantehely Mountains, which are a local spur of the Alleghany Mountains in North Carolina, just where that State touches Georgia and Tennessee." Bishop Elliott!

A single specimen of this very interesting species was found in the locality above mentioned, by Bishop Elliott, in whose cabinet I noticed it some months ago. In sculpture it is closely allied to *H. indentata* Say, of which it might almost be termed a gigantic variety, but the impressed striæ are more numerous, and closer together. The form of the aperture is very near that of *H. inornata* Binney.*

The general aspect of this shell reminds one of the Asiatic group, to which *H. resplendens* Phil. and *H. vitrinoides* Desh. belong.

XXXV.—*Remarks on certain Species of North American Helicidæ.*

By Thomas Bland.

Read February 22, 1858.

It appears not a little singular that many of the Helices of the United States are but imperfectly understood, and that much contrariety of opinion exists both there and in Europe

---

* This species is well known and understood, but I rather doubt its identity with *H. inornata* Say.

regarding them. This is particularly the case as to some of the species described by Thomas Say. To a considerable extent it may be attributed to the inaccessibility of Say's writings, now happily remedied by the recent publication of all relating to the terrestrial species by Mr. W. G. Binney.

Some of the species have been moreover hitherto rare, and seeing how much they vary, an extensive suite of specimens can alone enable a Conchologist to arrive at any satisfactory conclusion on points in dispute.

The valuable work of the late Dr. Amos Binney, only recently completed under the supervision of Dr. A. A. Gould, has added very much to our knowledge of the subject, but the text, written some years since, scarcely gives the information or the opinions as to several of the groups, which more recent study of them, and the present appreciation of the value of specific characters, would seem to demand and justify.

It is to be regretted that some of the specimens of the Land shells, deposited by Say at the Academy in Philadelphia, have been lost, and I fear that not all of those remaining are, strictly speaking, entirely reliable.

Mr. Isaac Lea has described a considerable number of species, and published figures of some of them, but the descriptions are generally by no means ample, and the figures not always satisfactory.

In Europe there has certainly been disregard of the writings of American authors, which, with the adoption there of Rafinesquean names, has added to the prevailing confusion.

Dr. Pfeiffer has published some grievous errors in his works, but has unquestionably been puzzled by the conflicting views of American Conchologists.

In reviewing the North American Land Shells, we must not overlook the fact, that in no part of the world have species such a wide distribution in latitude, owing it may be argued to the direction, from north to south, of the Rocky and Apalachian Mountain chains.

The fact of wide distribution of identical or closely allied forms is admitted, but how far attributable to the physical outlines of the Continent, or to circumstances connected with their original creation, are subjects of deep interest.*

Very many of the species present great variations,—so much so as to induce difference of opinion as to whether individuals should be considered simply varieties, or valid species. Our knowledge of the limits of variation is very circumscribed and unsatisfactory, and we know little or nothing of the causes of this variation,—whether due to physical circumstances or to creative power.

Several species have a tendency to run into, or are represented by acutely carinated forms; *H. alternata* Say is thus represented by *H. Cumberlandiana* Lea, *H. palliata* Say by *H. helicoides* Lea, *H. stenotrema* Fer. by *H. spinosa* Lea, and I may add *H. Troostiana* Lea by *H. fatigiata* Say. The metropolis of the carinated forms seems to be Tennessee.

The sculpturing and epidermis also greatly vary ; the fine incremental striæ of the Ohio *H. alternata*, are replaced in the South by strongly developed ribs, and in some individuals of *H. palliata*, the rough epidermis described by Say is wholly wanting. The situation of the teeth on the peristome is by no means constant, especially in *H. tridentata* Say.

A careful examination of the animals of the varieties of the species would be a most valuable contribution to science,—it would show to what extent variation in the shell prevails, without variation in its living tenant.

The local distribution of varieties renders it most important, in seeking to identify the species of Authors, to learn from whence their specimens were obtained, and to study examples from the same locality.

---

* It is worthy of remark, that in the limited area of the Island of Jamaica, the forms of *H. acuta* Lam. differ as widely as those of *H. alternata* Say, distributed over the North American continent from Canada to Texas.

Having enjoyed the advantage of much intercourse, as well personal as by correspondence, with Mr. W. G. Binney, to whose liberality I am greatly indebted for very many specimens, and also for information derived from his numerous correspondents, and from a study of his late father's papers, and cabinet, I desire to publish my views on some of the North American species (especially those described by Say), in the hope that they will at least aid in the elucidation of questions regarding them.

For the extensive suite of specimens in my cabinet I am under much obligation to many friends and correspondents, and particularly to Bishop Elliott. I would also acknowledge the very interesting and instructive correspondence had two years ago with Mr. R. J. Shuttleworth.

My thanks are due to my friend Mr. Edward Magens for the excellent figures on Plate ix. which illustrate this paper.

Helix fatigiata Say.

Plate IX. Fig. 17—20.

SYNONYMY.

Polygyra* *fatigiata Say* Diss. of Useful Knowledge, II. p. 229. 1829.
——— " Desc. of some new Terr. and Fluv. Shells
of N. Amer., p. 1. No. 3. 1840.
Helix *fatigiata Binn.* Bost. Jl. III., p. 388 ex parte (excl. Syn. et fig.)
1840.
——— *Texasiana var. B. Chemn.* ed. 2. Helix I., p. 86 (excl. desc. Syn.
et fig.). 1846.
——— " *β. Pfr.* Mon. Hel. I. No. 1086 (excl. desc. et Syn.).
1848.

---

* Mr. W. G. Binney informs me, that this specific name was written originally in Say's MS., *fastigiata.* Pfeiffer (Malak. Blatt. 1856) objects to *fatigiata* as not being a Latin word. The former would certainly be more correct, and was doubtless intended, but seeing that it has been used by Hutton for another species, I retain the latter.

Helix   *Dorfeuilliana Desh.* Fer. Hist. I. p. 73, tab. 69 D. fig. 3. (excl. Syn.).

—— *Texasiana Desh.* l. c. p. 74 (excl. desc. Syn. et fig.).

—— *fatigiata Binn.* Terr. Moll. II. p. 193, ex parte (excl. Syn.) pl. xxxix. fig. 4.   1851.

——   "   *Shuttl.* Diag. n. Moll. p. 17 (Bern. Mittheil.). 1852.

Polygyra   "   *W. G. Binn.* Reprint of Say's Descr. of Terr. Shells of N. Amer. p. 37.   1857.

In order to appreciate correctly Say's species, his remarkably lucid description and remarks should be carefully studied; for facility of reference I subjoin them:

"*Polygyra fatigiata.* Shell convex beneath, nearly plane above, the spire being hardly perceptibly elevated ; whorls a little over six, compressed, acutely carinated, crossed by numerous raised, equidistant lines, which form grooves between them ; superior surface not at all convex ; aperture subreniform ; labrum reflected, regularly arcuated, describing two-thirds of a circle ; within two toothed, lower tooth conic obtuse, superior tooth compressed, transverse, placed further within the aperture than the inner one, from which it is separated by a wide and deep and obvious sinus ; labrum with a very profound duplicature ; which has a concave surface, but with no emargination near its acute tip ; beneath exhibiting only two volutions, without any distinct groove on the external one near the suture ; beneath the carina the elevated lines are obsolete.

"Greatest breadth seven-twentieths of an inch.

"Found by Mr. Lesueur in the vicinity of New Harmony. It is very closely allied to that species which I described under the name of *plicata ;* the character of the mouth is very similar, but in that shell, such is the situation and form of the teeth of the labrum, that at first view they do not seem to be separated by a remarkable sinus, and the inferior tooth is compressed and larger than the other ; the duplicature of its labrum is emarginate near the tip. The present species is also larger, carinated, and the elevated lines are obsolete below the carina."

No doubt can exist as to the form indicated by Say under the above description, and it is strange that the species should have been so much misapprehended. A specimen deposited by Say in the Cabinet of the Academy of Nat. Sci. of Philadelphia is still preserved there,—it entirely agrees with his description, and with Binney's figure (Pl. xxxix. fig. 4.), in the "Terrestrial Mollusks."

Dr. Binney in the Bost. Jl. unites *fatigiata* with *H. plicata* Say, *H. Troostiana* Lea, and *H. Dorfeuilliana* Lea, adopting the first specific name, that of *plicata*, otherwise having priority, being preoccupied. His figure (Pl. xix. fig. 3) represents *Troostiana* Lea, a nearly allied form. The same views are expressed in the Terr. Moll. Binney gives there two figures, one (Pl. xxxix. fig. 4) of *fatigiata*, and the other (fig. 2) of *Troostiana* under the name of *plicata*.

Pfeiffer treats *fatigiata* Binn. (*H. Troostiana* Lea), *H. plicata* Say, and *H. fatigiata* Say, as synonyms of *H. Texasiana* Mor., which is certainly quite distinct,—adopts *H. Troostiana* Lea as a good species, and confounds *H. Dorfeuilliana* Lea with another species.

The same errors prevail in Chemnitz (ed. 2), and in Reeve's Conch. Icon., in neither of which works is *fatigiata* Say figured.

Deshayes (Fer. Hist.) has *fatigiata* Say, and *fatigiata* Binn. in his synonymy of *H. Texasiana* Mor., but describes and refers to a figure of the former, under the name of *Dorfeuilliana* Lea, of which he gives *plicata* Say as synonym. He refers to a specimen in Ferussac's collection, labelled *plicata* Say, but Say's name being preoccupied adopts *Dorfeuilliana* Lea, mentioning that he had himself proposed *finitima*. He admits the specific value of *Troostiana* Lea, with much doubt.

Shuttleworth (Bern. Mittheil.) points out the errors of Pfeiffer, correctly determines *fatigiata* Say, and *Dorfeuilliana* Desh., and also *Texasiana* Mor., but at the date of that publication misconceived *Dorfeuilliana* Lea, and *plicata* Say.

In justice to Mr. Shuttleworth I subjoin a copy of his accurate description, and of his observations; they are in a work not readily met with in' the United States, and I should add were not accepted by Pfeiffer in 1856 (vid. Malak. Blatt.).

HELIX FATIGIATA SAY.

"T. spurie umbilicato-perforata, superne plana, subtus inflato-convexa, acute carinata, plicato-striata, striis subtus exilioribus, corneo-rufescens, superne obscura, subtus nitidula; anfr. 6½, lente accrescentes, plani, ultimus ad aperturam brevissime deflexus et scrobiculato-constrictus, basi devius; sutura satis profunda; apertura subreniformis, valde coarctata; perist. albidum, reflexum, marginibus dente triangulari linguiformi profunde intrante junctis, dextro dente valido profunde immerso, basali dente minore submarginali munito.

"Diam. maj. 10, min. 9; alt. 3 mill.

"*Syn. Polygyra fatigiata* Say Descr. of some new Terr. and Fluv. Shells of N. Amer. p. 1. No. 3.
"*Helix Dorfeuilliana* Desh. in Fer. Hist., I. p. 73, et tab. 69 D. fig. 3.

"*Hab.*   Spec. ultra 12 e Tennessee misit Lequereux:
"*Obs.* Sub nomine H. Texasianæ 3 species a cl. Pfeiffer confusæ sunt.
" 1. H. fatigiata Binn., quæ ad H. Troostianam Lea (H. plicata Say), pertinet.
" 2. H. fatigiata Say, supra descripta.
" 3. H. Texasiana Mor., ad quam forsan tantum var. γ pertinet. Figura Kusteriana (Chemn., ed. 2. tab. 10. f. 11–12), ab H. Texasiana Mor., secundum exemplaria authentica in collectione Charpenteriana conservata, omnino abhorret, aut H. Troostianæ mala delineatio, aut species mihi omnino ignota est. H. Texasiana Mor. non valde ab H. Hindsi Pfr. discrepat. H. fatigiata Say differt ab H. Troostiana Lea, testa superne plana, acute carinata, dimensionibus majoribus, et dente supero majore et magis conspicuo : ab H. Texasiana Mor. testa superne plana, carinata et dente supero profunde inunerso, nec superficialiter in margine peristomatis sito."

H. fatigiata Say is larger than *Troostiana* Lea, *plicata* Say, and *Dorfeuilliana* Lea; it is most nearly allied to the first, and through it is connected with the second, but wholly distinct from the last. The parietal tooth is more rectangular than that of

Troostiana, in which it is slightly emarginate near the tip,—but much more so in *plicata,* while the parietal tooth in *Dorfeuilliana* is rather quadrate. The teeth on the peristome in *fatigiata* and *Troostiana* are much alike, as regards form, size, and position,—the superior one being the largest,—both are larger and transverse in *Dorfeuilliana* and in *plicata,* the inferior one being the largest in the latter. Behind the peristome there are two small pits, showing the situation of the teeth in *fatigiata* and *Troostiana,* while there is scarcely more than a deep, well marked constriction in *Dorfeuilliana.* H. *Troostiana* has a slight groove on the inner side of the last whorl, the absence of which in *fatigiata* is noticed by Say, but I scarcely consider that a good specific character. Fresh specimens of H. *fatigiata* are, I believe, covered with a very thin epidermis, on which hairs are sparingly scattered,—the scars of the hairs may be detected, especially on the last whorl, in denuded shells.

H. *fatigiata* has, at a short distance within the aperture on the base of the last whorl, a small, detached, erect, rounded tubercle, answering probably the same purpose in the economy of the animal, as the "fulcrum"* originally noticed by Mr. Lea (Observations Vol. V. p. 80) in H. *spinosa,* though of a different construction.

The measurements of my specimens agree with those given by Shuttleworth.

For further illustration of the differences in the species in question, I refer to the accompanying figures.

_____

* In his "Notes on American Land Shells" (Proc. Acad. Nat. Sc., Phila. Oct. 1857), Mr. W. G. Binney mentions having a specimen of *H. fallax* Say, in which there is "a well developed *fulcrum* as in *H. spinosa,* &c." I should explain that he received the specimen referred to from me (one of several given to me by Dr. Budd), and that it is by no means *H. fallax,*—rather a very large form of *H. vultuosa* Gould, or its close ally. In the latter species, as well as in Mr. Binney's shell, there is a short, somewhat transversely elongated tubercle, not rounded and obtuse, though in the same situation as in *H. fatigiata.* There is no such process in *H. fallax.*

For fine specimens of *H. fatigiata Say* from Tennessee, I am under obligation to the late Judge Tappan, and to Mr. J. G. Anthony.

Helix Troostiana Lea.

Plate IX. Fig. 21-23.

SYNONYMY.

Polygyra *Troostiana Lea* Trans. Am. Phil. Soc. VI. p. 107. Pl. xxiv.
.   fig. 119.   1838.
Helix *fatigiata Binn.* Bost. Jl. III. p. 388, ex parte (excl. Syn.)—pl.
            xix. fig. 3.   1840.
—— *Troostiana Pfr.* Mon. Hel. I. No. 1088.   1848.
——   "   *Desh.* in Fer. Hist. I. p. 75, tab. 69 D. fig. 4 ?
——   "   *Chemn.* ed. 2, Helix I. p. 376, tab. 65. fig. 21-24.
—— *fatigiata Binn.* Terr. Moll. II. p. 193 ex parte (excl. Syn.)   1851.
—— *plicata*   "   "   " III. tab. xxxix. fig. 2.
—— *Troostiana Rv.* Conch. Icon. Helix. No. 706. pl. cxx. fig. 702.
                                                   1852.
—— *plicata Shuttl.* Diag. n. Moll. p. 18 (Bern. Mitth.).   1852.

Lea's description and remarks are as follows :—for copies of his figures see Pl. IX. fig. 21, 22.

" POLYGYRA TROOSTIANA.

"T. superne subplanatâ, inferne subinflatâ, corneâ, longitudinaliter striatâ, late umbilicatâ ; anfr. 6 ; aperturâ lunatâ, tridentata.

"Shell above nearly flat, below somewhat inflated, horn color ; longitudinally striate, widely umbilicate ; whorls 6 ; aperture lunate, three toothed.

"*Habitat.*—Tennessee. Prof. Troost.

"Diam. .4, Length .2 of an inch.

"*Remarks.*—This species strongly resembles *P. Dorfeuilliana,* herein described, being nearly of the same size, and possessing most of its characters. It differs, however, in the large solid tooth on the left lip being more angular, and in the two teeth on the right lip being somewhat differently placed. In the striæ it differs much, these being larger, much better defined, and passing over the whorls. In the umbilicus it is wider, and shows more of the two whorls. This shell forms the fourth of a group, the form of the apertures of which is exceedingly alike, viz. *P. fatigiata* Say, *P. plicata* Say,* and *P. Dorfeuilliana* Nob."

As already mentioned, Binney gives a figure of this species in the Boston Jl. as *fatigiata* Say, and in the Terr. Moll. as *plicata* Say.

In Pfeiffer's Mon., in Chemnitz (ed. 2), and in Reeve's Conch. Icon. no doubt is expressed as to *Troostiana* being a good species. The figures in the two latter works appear certainly to be of Lea's shell.

Deshayes, in Fer. Hist., refers to its close affinity with his *Dorfeuilliana* (*fatigiata* Say), of which he is inclined to treat it as a variety,—the figure to which he refers (Pl. 69 D. fig. 4) is not altogether satisfactory.

Shuttleworth in Diag. n. Moll. (1852), as already quoted, erroneously considered *Troostiana* Lea identical with *plicata* Say, and in his observations on *H. Dysoni*,† in the same work, as scarcely more than a variety of *Dorfeuilliana* Lea, but he subsequently entertained a different opinion, as I shall presently explain.

Lea's description is unfortunately meagre, and his magnified figure, copied on Pl. IX. fig. 22, does not correctly show the parietal tooth,—its form, indeed, as figured, might be referred to *H. plicata*, but the size, form, and position of the two other teeth agree with *Troostiana*.

---

* Mr. Lea in his remarks on *H. Troostiana* and *H. Dorfeuilliana*, refers to *H. plicata* Say, but in fact alluded to *H. pustula* Fer., labelled *plicata* Say in his cabinet.

† For copy of the description and observations on this species see p. 295.

Mr. Lea has kindly allowed me to examine his original specimen, which differs from mine only in having the parietal tooth somewhat more emarginate.

H. Troostiana is very closely allied to *H. fatigiata* Say, from which I separate it with some hesitation. In its fresh state it has a thin, sparingly hirsute epidermis. I have moreover two specimens in my cabinet (both hirsute), which are as acutely carinated as *fatigiata*, with the striæ as prominent below as above,—(in one more numerous), but both having the parietal tooth of *Troostiana*.

I am not altogether satisfied with the validity of Shuttleworth's remark, that the superior tooth in *fatigiata* is larger and more conspicuous than in *Troostiana*.

This species has the same tubercle within the last whorl as *H. fatigiata.*

The following are the measurements of my specimens,—of one received from Judge Tappan, and agreeing with Mr. Lea's. Diam. maj. 8, min. 7, alt. 3.

Var. b.—carinata. Diam. maj. 9, min. 8, alt. 3.

Var. c.—minor. Carinate, and with striæ below more numerous than above—an additional one being intercalated between nearly every pair passing over the carina.

Diam. maj. 8, min. 7, alt. 3.

Mr. W. G. Binney, in his "Notes on American Land Shells," remarks on the plates in the "Terrestrial Mollusks" in the following terms,—" Helix plicata Say. Pl. xxxix. Fig. 2. Mr. Say's type is preserved in the collection of the Academy. Having carefully compared it with Mr. Lea's original *Troostiana*, I am led to believe them identical. In this case Mr. Lea's name alone will stand, as that of Mr. Say is pre-occupied." He adds, that of twenty-five specimens found in Tennessee by Bishop Elliott, " all were well marked *H. Troostiana.*" Since our recent discussion of this subject, and further careful study of the specimens referred to, Mr. Binney renounces the above opinion, believes with me that *H. Troostiana* Lea and *H. plicata* Say are distinct, and admits that the Bishop's specimens are of the latter species.

There is a good specimen of *H. Troostiana* Lea in the cabinet of the Academy, which was, I learn, received from Mr. Sowerby.

For examples of this species from Tennessee, I am indebted to the late Judge Tappan, and to Mr. Postell of St. Simon's Island, Ga.

Helix Hazardi.

Plate IX. Fig. 27–30.

SYNONYMY.

Polygyra *plicata Say* Jl. Acad. Nat. Sci. Phila. Vol. II. p. 161. 1821.
Helix *fatigiata Binn.* Bost. Jl. III. p. 388 ex parte (excl. Syn. et pl. xix. fig. 3). 1840.
—— *Texasiana Pfr.* Mon. Hel. I. p. 418 (excl. desc. et Syn.). 1848.
—— *Dorfenilliana Desh.* in Fer. Hist. I. p. 73 (excl. desc. Syn. et fig.).
—— *Texasiana Chem.* ed. 2 Helix. I. p. 85 (excl. desc. Syn. et fig).
—— *fatigiata Binn.* Terr. Moll. II. p. 193 ex parte (excl. pl. xxxix. fig. 2). 1851.
—— *plicata W. G. Binney* Reprint of Say's Desc. of Terr. Shells of N. Amer. 1856.
Polygyra *Troostiana W. G. Binney* Notes on Amer. Land Shells, Proc. Acad. Nat. Sci. Phila. p. 21. 1857.

The following is Say's description with which his explanatory remarks, accompanying the description of *H. fatigiata,* should be studied.

" *Polygyra plicata.*—Shell convex beneath, depressed above, spire slightly elevated ; whorls five, compressed, crossed by numerous raised, equidistant lines, which form grooves between them ; aperture subreniform, labrum reflected, regularly arcuated, describing two-thirds of a circle; within two-toothed, teeth not separated by a remarkable sinus; labrum with a profound duplicature, which terminates in an acute angle at the centre of the aperture; beneath exhibiting only two volutions, of which the external one is slightly grooved near the suture.

"Inhabits Alabama. Breadth one-fourth of an inch. Cabinet of the Academy.

"This species is about the same size as *P. avara*,* but, besides other characters, it is sufficiently distinguished by the acute fold of the labrum. It was sent to the Academy by Mr. Samuel Hazard."

No author appears to have correctly identified this species. If distinct, as I fully believe it to be, the name must be changed, inasmuch as *H. plicata* Born is of prior date. Mr. W. G. Binney informs me that in Say's MS. there is an erased remark as to the name being pre-occupied, and proposing *beta*. As Pfeiffer has already trespassed on the Greek alphabet, I would suggest the propriety of dedicating the species to its discoverer, Mr. Hazard.

This shell may be distinguished from *fatigiata* Say, and *Troostiana* Lea, independently of the absence of the carina, by its smaller size, and more particularly by the different form, relative size, and position of the teeth. In those species the superior tooth on the peristome is transverse, compressed, and larger than the inferior one, from which it is separated by a "remarkable sinus," distinctly visible on looking into the aperture; the inferior tooth is obtuse. Immediately behind the peristome, the position of the teeth is marked by small

---

* Say describes *P. avara* as having 4 whorls, covered with numerous short robust hairs, and with no groove on the last whorl. He gives a quarter of an inch as the breadth. This is very different to the shells generally bearing the name of *avara*. I have one specimen in my cabinet, given to me by Dr. Budd, which agrees closely with Say's description.

shallow pits, giving the character to the last whorl designated by Shuttleworth " *scrobiculato-constrictus*,"—the striæ run over the whorl up to the peristome. In *H. Hazardi*, the two teeth on the peristome are of the same character as the superior one in *fatigiata* and *Troostiana*,—the inferior tooth is however the largest, and so partially conceals the lower margin of the superior one as to obstruct the view into the aperture, and give no appearance of separation " by a remarkable sinus." Both the teeth are more deeply seated than in the other species. The nature of the scrobiculation behind the peristome in *H. Hazardi* alone sufficiently distinguishes it from its allies. The space behind the peristome, and between it and the curved pit, showing the seat of the superior tooth, is convex and smooth, the striæ not extending over it. This character, as well as the form of the parietal and other teeth, is shown in Plate IX. fig. 27, 28.

This species has, in common with *fatigiata* Say and *Troostiana* Lea, a thin, brown, but more sparingly hirsute epidermis. I have noticed the tubercle within the last whorl, near the aperture, in *fatigiata* and *Troostiana*, but no such process exists in the species now under consideration. In *H. Hazardi*, the inferior tooth of the labrum, at its inner end, is continued back within the aperture, forming a white erect lamella on the floor of the whorl, parallel with, and leaving a narrow sinus between it and the inner wall, to which it is joined at its extremity, about 2½ mill. from the edge of the peristome. The position of this lamella can be seen through the shell.

In my remarks on *H. fatigiata* I have referred to the character of the parietal tooth in this species.

The size of my specimens is constant, viz., Diam., maj. 7, min. 6, alt. 3 mill.

In the Cabinet of the Academy at Philadelphia there are three specimens (dead shells), labelled *H. plicata* Say, and with memorandum on the label that they were deposited by Say. The habitat given is Kentucky. These specimens agree

entirely with Bishop Elliott's, from one of which my figures
were taken.

For the beautiful specimens in my cabinet, I am indebted to
Bishop Elliott, who collected them in Murray Co., Georgia,
and Soquatchee Valley, Tenn. He has recently sent me also,
" the only one found in a pretty extensive search in the Cumberland Mountains, Tennessee."

Helix Dorfcuilliana Lea.

Plate IX. Fig. 24–26.

Polygyra *Dorfcuilliana* Lea Trans. Amer. Phil. Soc. VI. p. 107, pl.

          xxiv. fig. 118.   1838.
Helix *fatigiata Binn.* Bost. Jl. III. p. 388 ex parte. (excl. Syn. et fig.)

                                                           1840.
——   "   "   . Terr. Moll. II. p. 193 ex parte. (excl. Syn. et

          fig.)   1851.

(non Pfr.—Desh. in Fer. Hist.—Chemn.—Reeve.)

The following is a copy of Mr. Lea's description,—his figures
are copied on Plate IX. fig. 24, 25.

" POLYGYRA DORFEUILLIANA.

"T. superne obtuso-conicà, inferne subinflatâ, nitidâ, corneâ, longitu-
linaliter striatâ, late umbilicatâ ; anfr. 6 ; aperturâ lunatâ, tridentatâ.

" Shell above obtusely conical, below somewhat inflated, shining, horn
color ; longitudinally striate, widely umbilicate ; whorls six ; aperture
lunate, three toothed.

" *Hab.*—Ohio. Mr. Dorfeuille, Cincinnati.
" Diam. .3 ; Length .2 of an inch.

" *Remarks.*—I adopt Mr. Say's genus *Polygyra*, believing the divi-
sion, though very artificial, quite as good as many made by Lamarck.

This species has, like *P. fatigiata* Say and *P. plicata* Say, one large tooth on the left lip, and two smaller ones on the right lip. It differs from the first in not being carinate, from the last in being larger, and having larger striæ. In the *Dorfeuilliana* the tooth on the left lip is large and square, with an indentation in the centre. The view into the mouth is nearly obstructed by the teeth, leaving, to appearance, three nearly square apertures. The superior part of the shell is striate, while the inferior part is nearly smooth, and exhibits two volutions. I have seen but a single specimen, which, I believe, is the only one obtained by Mr. Dorfeuille, who obligingly sent it to me."

I have already mentioned that Binney, both in the Boston Jl. and Terr. Moll., treats this species as identical with *fatigiata* Say, *plicata* Say, and *Troostiana* Lea, and that Deshayes confounds it with the two former.

Lea's *Dorfeuilliana* is certainly not described in Pfeiffer, Chemnitz (ed. 2), or Reeve, nor is there any figure of it in the two latter works. In all of them Honduras is erroneously given as one of the habitats, and I believe that they describe and figure the Honduras species, referred to by Shuttleworth (Diag. N. Moll. p. 16), in the following terms :—

" HELIX DYSONI.

" T. late et subperspective umbilicata, depressa, nitida, rufo-cornea, superne brevissime conoidea, plicato-striata, subtus inflata, striis exilioribus subobsoletis, lineisque paucis interruptis spiralibus circa umbilicum impressis obscure notata ; anfr. 5½, convexiusculi, lente accrescentes, ultimus vix descendens, angulatus ; sutura profunda ; apertura majuscula, auriformis, tridentata : dente 1, valido, obliquo, pliciformi, in pariete aperturali intrante ; perist. reflexum, album, dentibus 2 marginalibus intus munitum.

" *Syn. Helix Dorfeuilliana* Pfr. l. c. p. 410, No. 1067, non Lea. et excl. fig. Fer.
     ——   "   "   Chemn. ed. 2, t. 65, fig. 25–28.

" *Hab.*—In Honduras (Dyson).

" *Obs.*—Spec. 6 vidi. Species nullo modo cum H. Dorfeuilliana Lea confundenda, quæ, ultimo anfractu subtus devio umbilicum tantum spurium et rimalem ostendente, revera solummodo perforata est. Differt insuper H. Dorfeuilliana Lea, dente parietali magno, fere tetragono, linguiformi, peristomatis margina jungendo. H. Dorfeuilliana Lea (ad specimen unicum descripta) vix nisi H. Troostiana Lea varietas. H. Dysoni H. fallaci et Hopetonensi proxime affinis videtur."

Shuttleworth gives no measurements.

In January, 1856, Mr. Shuttleworth wrote to me, acknowledging receipt of some shells sent to him for examination, and which I had not then determined.

As to one, agreeing with my figure 26 on Pl. ix., he said, " this is *H. Dorfeuilliana* Lea, which I had never seen, but I find Albers has it unnamed from Texas, and I was on the point of describing it as a new species, so little does Lea's figure agree." The shell referred to may be a variety of Lea's species, to which certainly it is allied; it is distinct, however, from *fatigiata*, *Troostiana*, and *Hazardi*.

With respect to another shell, the same as my figure 25 *a.* Pl. ix., Shuttleworth remarked, " this is, I suppose, the true *H. plicata* Say, but not being able to compare Say's description, I am not sure,—it is at all events distinct from *H. Dorfeuilliana* Lea, *fatigiata* Say, and *Troostiana* Lea."

I find on examination of Mr. Lea's original specimen of *Dorfeuilliana*, that it entirely agrees with the form supposed by Mr. Shuttleworth to be *plicata* Say. The magnified figure of the aperture (Pl. ix. fig. 25 *a.*), taken from a specimen in my cabinet, agrees nearly with Mr. Lea's figure (Pl. ix. fig. 25).

Pfeiffer refers in the Synonymy of his *Dorfeuilliana* to the figures in Chemnitz and Reeve, of which I annex copies (Pl. ix. fig. 31, 32), in order to show how widely they differ from Lea's species, and inasmuch as Shuttleworth refers to the former figure in his Synonymy of *H. Dysoni.* Reeve, in ex-plantation of his figure, says,—" the specimen here figured has no teeth on the inner wall of the aperture, it being as com-monly absent as present." I have examined many specimens of Lea's shell, and have seen none without the parietal tooth.

Pfeiffer also refers, but with doubt, to the figure in Fer. Hist. t. 69 D. fig. 3, which is, as I have shown, *H. fatigiata* Say, and in Mon. III. p. 264, he increases the confusion by adding *H. finitima* Desh. (*plicata* Say) to the Synonymy of *Dorfeuilliana* Lea.

It may be noticed that Honduras, and the habitats 'in the United States of Lea's species, are in distinct zoological pro-vinces,—I do not know any species of *Helix* common to both.

H. Dorfeuilliana Lea differs materially in its characters from the three preceding species ; the striæ on the upper sur-face are not so well defined as in *Troostiana*, but more so than in *Hazardi*, while the base is more smooth than in either of them, having only very delicate striæ, with microscopic im-pressed spiral lines.

The parietal tooth is quadrate,—the two teeth on the right lip are more nearly of the same size and form than in *fatigiata* and *Troostiana*. In this species the inferior tooth is transverse, and in some specimens broader than the superior one, but has a somewhat pointed apex,—both are very nearly equally deeply seated, but so far apart as to allow a view between them into the aperture, leaving, as Mr. Lea expresses it, " to appearance three nearly square apertures." Say would have described the two teeth as "separated by a remarkable sinus." The peristome of this is more thickened and less reflected than in the other species,—behind it is deeply constricted, without any appearance of pits showing the position of the teeth within.

H. Dorfeuilliana Lea varies in size,—the following are the measurements of my largest and smallest specimens :—

Diam. maj. 8, min. 7, alt. 3½ mill.

"   "   6½   "   5½   "   3   "

With respect to the shell considered by Shuttleworth to be II. *Dorfeuilliana*, it will be seen from the figure (Pl. ix. fig. 26), which differs, as he says, from Lea's, that the superior tooth on the labrum is larger and more deeply seated than the inferior one, and that the latter, though more developed, is much of the same form as the inferior tooth in *fatigiata* and *Troostiana*. The parietal tooth partakes of the general character of that in Lea's type of *Dorfeuilliana*, but its lower and terminal margins project more perpendicularly from the parietal wall. The umbilical perforation is also larger, and the base of the shell is more smooth.

The following are the measurements of a large specimen :—

Diam. maj. 9, min. 8, alt. 4.

I am much inclined to consider this a distinct species, but remark upon it, as I believe it is more commonly found in cabinets under the name of *Dorfeuilliana*, than the shell described by Lea.

II. Dorfeuilliana, and also the shell last considered, have a tubercle within, very similar to that in *fatigiata* and *Troostiana*.

Both forms were given to me, neither separated nor determined, by Mr. J. G. Anthony, with Kentucky as habitat.

This species does not inhabit Ohio,—Mr. Dorfeuille resided at Cincinnati, but there must have been some mistake as to the habitat of the specimen sent to Mr. Lea.

NOTE.—*H. Texasiana* Mor., with which Pfeiffer and other authors confound Say's above named species, is very distinct, especially in the form of the parietal and other teeth,—the two on the peristome are moreover on its margin. I publish a copy of Moricand's magnified figure (Plate ix. fig. 33), and also Reeve's figure (same plate, fig. 34), which fairly represents the species.

H. Texasiana, in the form of the aperture and teeth, is nearly allied to *H. Hindsi* Pfr., and certainly more to *H. ventrosula* Pfr. than to *H. fatigiata* Say, or *Hazardi* Nob. (*plicata* Say).

The figures in Chem. (ed. 2, t. 10, fig. 11–12) said to be of *H. Texasiana*, and to which Shuttleworth refers in his observations on *H. fatigiata* (see ante, p. 286), appear to represent an undescribed species from Louisiana, of which I have specimens from the cabinet of Dr. Binney, and also from Mr. Isaac Lea.

In my cabinet there are numerous specimens of *H. Texasiana* Mor. from Texas and Mexico,—received from Judge Tappan, Dr. Newcomb, and Mr. W. G. Binney. One from Tamaulipas has the rufous band on the periphery, agreeing with Pfeiffer's Var. γ.

Helix Pennsylvanica Green.

SYNONYMY.

Helix *Pennsylvanicus Green* Cont. to Macl. Lyc. N. 1, p. 8.   1827.
——— *Pennsylvanica Binn.* Bost. Jl. I. p. 483, pl. 16.   1837.
———   "   *De Kay*, N. Y. Moll. p. 41, pl. 3, fig. 45.   1843.
———   "   *Pfr.* Mon. Hel. I. No. 759, ex parte.   1848.
———   "   *Chemn.* ed. 2 Helix No. 442, ex parte, t. 73, fig. 4–5.
——— *Mitchelliana Desh.* in Fer. Hist. p. 137. ex parte. t. 97, fig. 4–7. nec. 13–16.
——— *Pennsylvanica Binn.* Ter. Moll. II. p. 105. Pl. VII.   1851.
———   "   *Rv.* Conch. Icon. No. 676 ex parte, Pl. CXVII. fig. 676.   1852.

Green's description is not readily met with, even in the United States, and I subjoin a copy of it:—

"H. PENNSYLVANICUS.

Shell subglobose; spire elevated; whorls 6 or 7, with numerous oblique wrinkles or striæ; suture deeply impressed; epidermis smooth, and of an olive-brown color, like most of the American Helices; umbilicus closed, or masked; aperture slightly contracted at the base,—a small callosity on the inner margin of the other lip near its lower angle. Shell rather more than half an inch in diameter.

This shell somewhat resembles the *H. clausa* of Mr. Say, but may very readily be distinguished from that species by the closed umbilicus, the number of its whorls, and its general form. This shell is not uncommon in the moist ground near Chartier's Creek, in Washington Co., Pa. I obtained five or six specimens with but very little trouble at that locality, associated with the *H. solitaria, profunda,* and *palliata.*

Authentic specimens are in the Cabinet of the Academy at Philadelphia.

This species has not been accurately determined by European authors, who have confounded it with *II. clausa* Say and *II. Mitchelliana* Lea, from which, however, it is entirely distinct. Green's description, to be found only in a scarce work, has probably been unknown, but the shell was correctly described and figured by Binney in the Boston Journal.

Pfeiffer, nevertheless, has *II. clausa* in the Synonymy of *II. Pennsylvanica,* and refers to Say's figure of the former, as well as to Binney's of the latter.

The confusion has been increased by American Conchologists, who have treated, in my opinion erroneously, *II. clausa* Say and *II. Mitchelliana* Lea as identical. It may also be remarked that Dr. Jay, in his Catalogue, 2d ed. (1836), admitted *Pennsylvanica* and *clausa* to be distinct, but in the 4th ed. (1852) adopted the views of Pfeiffer.

Shuttleworth, in 1853, published (for private distribution only I believe), figures of many North American species, and among them, of *II. Pennsylvanica* and *II. Mitchelliana,* but each under the specific name of the other. He was evidently misled as to the latter by Lea's description, and misapprehended the former, not having seen that of Green.

Reeves' figure fairly represents this species, but he has the same error with regard to *II. clausa* as Pfeiffer.

Deshayes, in Fer. Hist., describes *H. Mitchelliana*, but refers to the figure, which is rather of *Pennsylvanica.*

The species under consideration may be readily distinguished from *clausa* and *Mitchelliana* by its somewhat triangular aperture, which is more like that of *H. elevata* Say; it is more elevated, has usually 6 whorls, more convex, and with deeper suture than in *H. clausa.* In mature shells the inner margin of the peristome, near the columella, has a tooth-like callus, very similar to that often prevailing in forms of *H. zaleta* Say, *thyroidus* Say, and *albolabris* Say. The umbilicus is invariably more or less open in *H. clausa*, but closed in *H. Pennsylvanica* and *Mitchelliana.*

This shell varies in size. The following are the dimensions of the largest and smallest specimens in my Cabinet:

Diam. maj. 19, min. 16½, alt. 11, mill.

    "   "   16,   "   14½,   "   9,   "

The distribution of this species is far more limited than that of *H. clausa.* I have seen specimens only from Pennsylvania, Ohio, and Illinois; but of *clausa* from Ohio, Kentucky, Tennessee, Alabama, Illinois, Iowa, and Missouri.

The mention of this and other species by De Kay in the New York Fauna, because of the probability of their discovery in that State, is calculated to mislead.

HELIX ELLIOTTI REDFIELD.

This species was described by Mr. John H. Redfield, in Annals of Lyceum Vol. VI, p. 170. Figures are now given on Pl. IX., figs. 8–10.

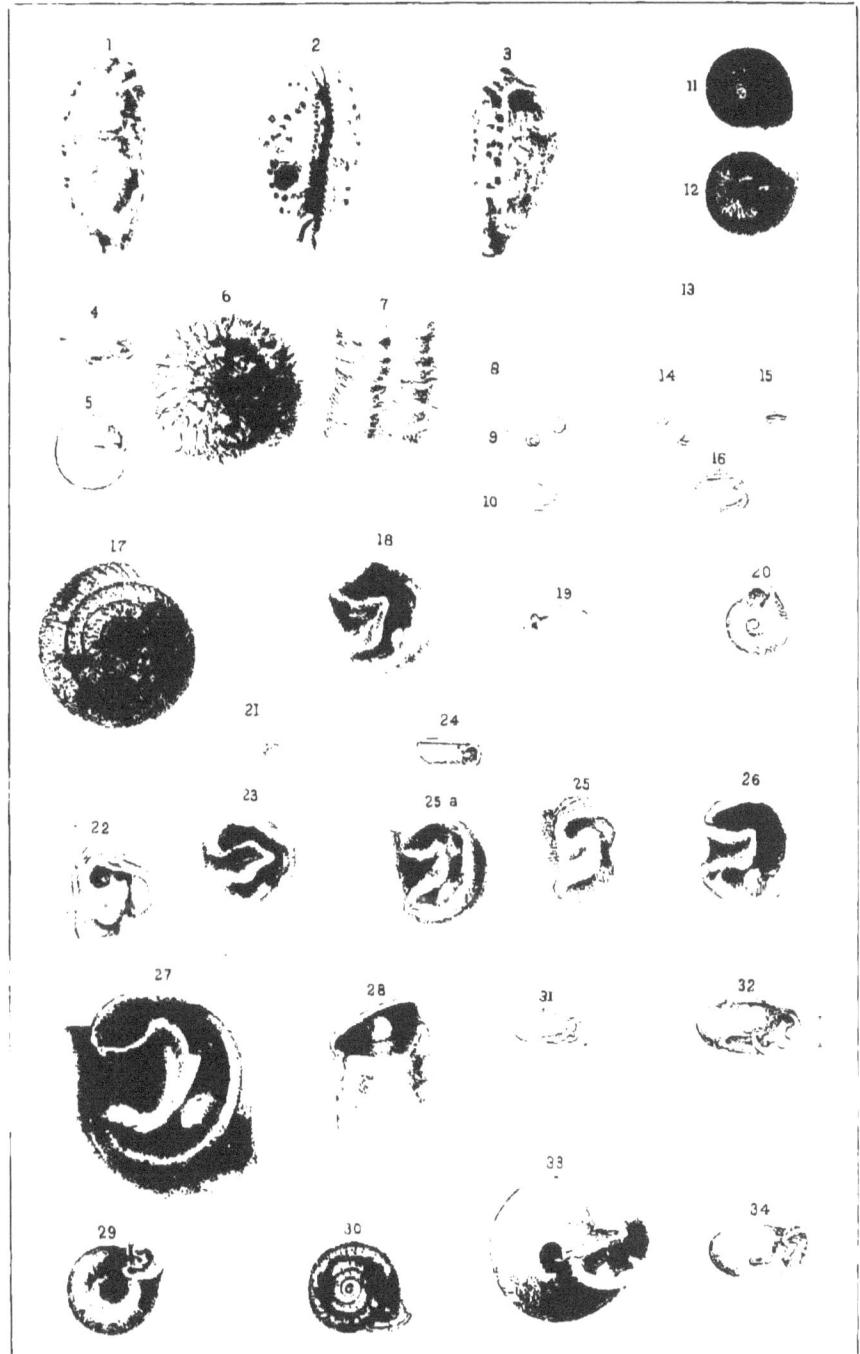

REMARKS

ON

CERTAIN SPECIES

OF

NORTH AMERICAN HELICIDÆ,

WITH

DESCRIPTIONS OF NEW SPECIES.

BY

THOMAS BLAND, F.G.S., LONDON,

MEMBER OF THE LYCEUM OF NATURAL HISTORY, NEW YORK; CORRESPONDING MEMBER OF THE
ACADEMY OF NATURAL SCIENCES, PHILADELPHIA, &c.

REPRINTED FROM THE ANNALS OF THE LYCEUM OF NATURAL HISTORY,
NEW YORK. VOL. VII.

PART II.

NEW YORK:

H. BAILLIÈRE, 440 BROADWAY.

LONDON:—H. BAILLIÈRE, 219 REGENT STREET.

PARIS:—J. B. BAILLIÈRE ET FILS, RUE HAUTEFEUILLE.

MADRID:—C. BAILLY-BAILLIÈRE, CALLE DEL PRINCIPE.

1860.

CONTENTS.

DESCRIPTIONS OF NEW SPECIES.

REMARKS ON THE FOLLOWING SPECIES, VIZ.:

[The Plate referred to will be issued with the next and concluding Part.]

Helix clausa Say.

SYNONYMY.

Helix *clausa Say* Jour. Acad. Phila. II. p. 154,   1821.
—— " " Amer. Conch. No. 4, pl. 37, fig. 1,   1832.
—— " *Binney* Bost. Jl. I. p. 482, pl. 15,   1837.
—— " *De Kay* N. Y. Moll. p. 31, ex parte,   1843.
—— *Pennsylvanica Pfr.* Mon. I. No. 759, ex parte,   1848.
—— " *Chem.* ed. 2, Helix No. 442, ex parte.
—— *Mitchelliana* " " " " 332, t. 56, fig. 6–8.
—— *clausa Binney* Terr. Moll. II. p. 107, ex parte, pl. 4,   1851.
Helix *Pennsylvanica Reeve* Conch. Ic. No. 676, ex parte,   1852.
—— *clausa W. G. Binney* Reprint of Say's Desc. p. 17,   1856.
(non Ferussac.)

Say thus described this species in the Journal of the Academy:—

" II. CLAUSA.
" Shell fragile, slightly perforated, subglobular, yellowish horn color, above convex; whorls four or five; aperture slightly contracted by the lip ; lip reflected, flat, white, nearly covering the umbilicus.

" Inhabits Illinois. Greatest breadth from one-half to three-fifths of an inch.

" A small but handsome species, which somewhat resembles *albola-bris*, but is much smaller, more rounded, and is subumbilicate. This shell also occurs, though perhaps rarely, in Pennsylvania."

I have already noticed that this species has been confounded by European authors with *H. Pennsylvanica* Green, and by those of America with *H. Mitchelliana* Lea.

H. clausa Say varies in form, size, and sculpture. Specimens in my cabinet from Selma, Ala., received from Mr. J. G. Anthony, may be described as rather strong than fragile, not shining or pellucid, the umbilicus only about half covered by the reflected lip, depressed rather than subglobular; the shell as strongly striate above and below, as *H. Pennsylvanica.*

I add the measurements of the largest and smallest individuals:

Diam. maj. 18, min. 15, Alt. 10 mill. anfr. 6.
"   "   12, "   10, "   7 "   " 5.

A specimen from Iowa is very similar to those from Alabama.

From Wisconsin, Missouri, Illinois, and Kentucky, I have forms which agree closely with Say's description,—in these the reflected lip is less thickened, the aperture is more round, the last whorl being more globose,—the umbilicus is more nearly covered, and the striæ are less prominent, especially at the base, than in the Alabama shells.

The measurement of an average sized specimen is :—
Diam. maj. 17, min. 15, Alt. 10 mill. anfr. 5.

Specimens from Tennessee, for which I am indebted to Mr. Postell, are small, extremely thin and pellucid, with the umbilicus generally but little open, the last whorl obsoletely angulated at the periphery.

Diam. maj. 14, min. 12, Alt. 8 mill. anfr. 5.

There is a variety figured by Mr. Shuttleworth (in the plates referred to in my notes on *H. Pennsylvanica*) as *H. clausa Say, var. subalbolabris.* It is, I believe, the globose form, with wider and less thickened lip, and more open umbilicus than in the Illinois shell. I have a specimen about equal in size to the largest one from Alabama,—it is pellucid, shining, and at the base nearly smooth, but showing the fine spiral impressed lines as distinctly as *H. Mitchelliana.* I received it from Ohio.

In the cabinet of the Academy at Philadelphia, there are three shells, understood to be those deposited by Say, labelled *H. clausa* Say, with Ohio as habitat, in the hand-writing of Mr. Phillips. These specimens agree pretty closely with Say's description.

The Alabama shells may be compared in *general aspect*, with

H. Pennsylvanica, and the others above mentioned with *H. Mitchelliana.* Say's *figure* is rather of the former,—his *description* and the figures of Dr. Binney of the latter forms.

In the Boston Journal, Dr. Binney describes the umbilicus as " nearly covered by the reflected lip,"—probably he had not then seen the imperforate *H. Mitchelliana,* as no reference is made to it.

He remarks in the " Terrestrial Mollusks," that the surface of *H. clausa* is " shining and its striæ of increase delicate and regular,"—also that " the umbilicus in specimens entirely mature is covered, but, as commonly seen, a small opening still remains." It would seem that Dr. B. did not know the Alabama variety, and alluded, when writing of the covered umbilicus, to *H. Mitchelliana* Lea, which he puts in the synonymy of *H. clausa.*

Mr. W. G. Binney, in his " Notes on American Land Shells " (Phil. Proc. 1857), states that the outline figures in Terr. Moll. (Pl. 4) do not represent *H. clausa ;* they are, however, very like my small Alabama or Tennessee specimens.

De Kay describes *H. clausa* as having the umbilicus occasionally entirely covered ; and states, erroneously, that it may be considered as a Southern species, extending to New Jersey and New York.

Reeve's figure of *H. clausa* (fig. 676), I have already referred to as being *H. Pennsylvanica.* He gives another (fig. 694), which may be the var. *subalbolabris,* but is more like *H. bucculenta* Gould, without the parietal tooth.

Helix Mitchelliana Lea.

SYNONYMY.

Helix *Mitchelliana Lea* Am. Phil. Trans. VI. 87, pl. 23, f. 71,   1836.
—— *clausa De Kay* N. Y. Moll. p. 31, ex parte, pl. 2, f. 13 ?   1843.

Helix *Mitchelliana Pfr.* Mon. I., No. 760,   1848.
——   "   *Desh.* in Fer. Hist. ex parte? excl. fig.
—— *clausa Binney* Terr. Moll. p. 107, ex parte, 1851.

The following is Mr. Lea's description :—

" H. MITCHELLIANA.

" T. superne obtuso-conicâ, inferne inflatâ, longitudinaliter et subtiliter striatâ, corneâ, diaphanâ, imperforatâ, anfr. 5 ; aperturâ subrotundatâ ; labro reflexo ; columellâ lævi.

" Shell above obtusely conical, below inflated, longitudinally and finely striate ; horn color, transparent, imperforate ; whorls 5 ; aperture nearly round ; outer lip reflexed ; columella smooth.

"*Remarks :* I am indebted to Dr. Mitchell for this shell, which was sent to him by a friend from Ohio. It is rather larger than the *H. clausa* Say, and *H. jejuna* Say, but in form resembles them. It may be distinguished from the latter in not being perforate, and from the former in having a sharper lip. In its striæ it is distinct from both, in having them larger and much better defined.

" *Hab.* Ohio. Diam. 7. Length .4 of an inch."

Lea's description agrees fairly with the shell now known in our cabinets as *H. Mitchelliana.*

Looking at his " Remarks," however, I cannot wonder at the many doubts which have arisen as to the shell intended to be indicated, inasmuch as the comparison with *H. clausa* and *H. jejuna* scarcely admits of satisfactory explanation.

The fact is, that Lea misapprehended both species, as I learn from correspondence with him,—he had in his cabinet under the latter name, a small form of *H. clausa*, and I have reason to believe that a variety, with imperfectly developed lip, of the very shell which he was about to describe as *H. Mitchelliana*, represented the former species. The language used by Lea shows that he referred to an *imperforate* shell as *H. clausa.*

H. Mitchelliana is certainly very closely allied to *H. clausa*, especially the form *described* by Say, but in Lea's species the umbilicus is entirely closed, and at the base the spiral impressed lines are more distinct, in which respect it agrees with *H. clausa* var. *subalbolabris*, to which I have already referred.

In *H. clausa* the umbilical region is more widely excavated, and the groove, behind the reflected lip, producing the contraction of the aperture, is continued at the base of the shell, becoming wider as it joins the umbilical opening. In *H. Mitchelliana* the groove is almost obliterated at the point of reflection of the lip over the umbilicus, by the more tumid character of the last whorl.

All the specimens in my cabinet of *H. Mitchelliana* are from Ohio.

The size is somewhat variable. I add the measurements of the largest and smallest individuals:—

Diam. maj. 17, min. 14, Alt. 9½, mill.
"   "   15, "   13, "   9   "

Helix jejuna Say.

SYNONYMY.

Helix *jejuna* Say Jour. Acad. N. Sci. Phila. II. p. 158,   1821.
—— *Mobiliana Lea* Proc Am. Phil. Soc. II. p. 82,   1841.
——   "   " Obs. IV. p. 17.
——*jejuna De Kay* N. Y. Moll. p. 46,   1843.
—— *Mobiliana Pfr.* Mon. L No. 844,   1848.
——   "   *Binney* Terr. Moll. II. p. 172, pl. 42, fig. 2,   1851.
——*jejuna W. G. Binney* Reprint Say's Descr. p. 19,   1856.

Say's description is as follows:—

" HELIX JEJUNA.

"Shell subglobular, glabrous, pale reddish brown; volutions five, slightly wrinkled, regularly rounded; spire convex; suture rather deeply impressed; aperture dilate lunate; labrum a little incrassated within, not reflected; umbilicus open, small.

"Breadth rather more than one-fifth of an inch. Inhabits the Southern States.

" Animal—light reddish brown, with a granular surface, longer than the breadth of the shell ; oculiferous tentacula elongated, and rather darker than the body.

" This shell is very closely allied to *H. sericea* of Southern Europe, but it differs from that species in being destitute of the hirsute vesture. I found several specimens of *jejuna*, during an excursion some time since into East Florida, at the Cow Fort on St. John River. It is in the collection of the Academy."

This species has not hitherto been identified, and unfortunately no authentic specimen of it is now to be found in the Cabinet of the Academy.

In the letter from Dr. Griffith to Dr. Binney, quoted at page 43, the former mentions having specimens of a shell given to him by Mr. Lea for *jejuna*, but not answering Say's description.   Mr. Lea, in his descriptions of *H. Mitchelliana* and *H. Mobiliana*, refers to *H. jejuna*, but admits, as I have already stated, having had under the latter name *H. clausa* Say.

It is singular that no allusion to *H. jejuna* is made by Dr. Binney in the " Terrestrial Mollusks," excepting by name only, in the lists in the first volume showing the geographical distribution of species.

Pfeiffer, not knowing the species, copies Say's description. In a letter, however, received by Mr. W. G. Binney from Pfeiffer, in the early part of the present year, he asks, " might not *H. Mobiliana* Lea be identical with the lost *H. jejuna* Say ?"

I believe that the question may safely be answered in the affirmative; indeed I do not hesitate to accord to Dr. Pfeiffer the merit of having discovered the lost species.

Lea's description of his species is as follows :—

" H. MOBILIANA.

" T. subglobosâ, rufo-corneâ, nitidâ, perforatâ, spirâ brevi, obtusâ ; suturis impressis ; anfr. 6, convexis; aperturâ lunatâ ; labro reflexo.

" Shell subglobose, reddish horn color, shining, perforate ; spire short, obtuse, sutures impressed, whorls 6, convex; aperture lunate; lip reflected. Diam. .30, length .25 of an inch.

" *Hab.* Vicinity of Mobile, Ala.

" *Remarks.* In form it is somewhat like *H. jejuna* Say, but is not one-fourth its size, and differs in color. There is rather a deep groove behind the lip, which is reddish. The umbilicus is small."

It will be seen on comparing the descriptions of *H. jejuna* and *H. Mobiliana* that they agree pretty closely, the principal difference being that the former is said to have a non-reflected, and the latter a reflected lip.

Dr. Binney (in Terr. Moll.) very accurately describes Lea's species; he says, " lip white, very narrow, reflected, a deep groove behind it; aperture well rounded, semicircular, considerably contracted by the impressed groove behind the lip, and a corresponding testaceous deposit, or rib, within." He remarks in addition : " a great part of the specimens have the aperture in a much less developed condition, the lip being acute, or the reflection but partly completed, and the depression behind the lip not visible."

I have many specimens of *H. Mobiliana,* collected in the old Cemetery at Savannah, by Bishop Elliott, and on St. Simon's Island, by Mr. Postell; in none can the lip be said to be, in the ordinary acceptation of the term, *reflected,* excepting slightly at the base of the aperture, and by the umbilicus.

With respect to the animal of *H. Mobiliana,* Mr. Postell has favored me with the following note : " Animal longer than the shell, very light yellowish ; granulate ; superior tentacles very dark, almost black, with a dark brown stripe running along the body, from the base of each ; inferior tentacles much shorter, of same color as the body." This description agrees to a considerable extent with Say's *H. jejuna.* I attach very little importance to the difference in color of the body of the animal.

Lea describes the species as having six whorls. I have not seen any specimen from the habitat assigned by him, but all in my cabinet have from four and a half to five whorls.

In the Spring of the present year I received many interesting shells from Mr. O. M. Dorman, collected by him at St. Augustine, and on the St. John's River, Florida, in the neighbourhood of the Cow Ford,* mentioned by Say. Among them were several very young shells, which I was unable to determine. Subsequently I had from the same gentleman additional specimens, more, but not fully, mature, yet sufficiently so to enable me to identify them with certainty as _H. Mobiliana._

This shell in its fresh state has a very delicate epidermis, having a silky lustre. The lower half of the first and part of the second whorl have microscopic raised spiral lines, which I have detected in the specimens received from Bishop Elliott and Mr. Dorman.

The size is variable, viz. :—

Diam. maj. 8, min. 7, Alt. 5½ mill. anfr. 5, Savannah.
"   " 6, " 5, " 4 "   " 4½ St. Simon's Is.
"   " 7, " 6, " 4 "   " 5 St. John's River.

Helix porcina Say.

Synonymy.

Helix _porcina Say_ Long's 2d Exped. to St. Peter's River, II. p. 257,
    pl. 15, fig. 2.   1824.
—— _hirsuta Binney_ Terr. Moll. II. p. 150 (_young_),   1851.

Say's description is as follows :—

" H. porcina.

" Shell depressed, yellowish brown ; epidermis rugose, with minute, very numerous bristles ; whorls rather more than four, depressed above, beneath rounded, forming a very obtuse angle rather above the centre of the whorl ; umbilicus open, rather small, profound ; labrum simple.

---

* Say speaks of the " Cow Fort," but I believe that Mr. Dorman's designation of the locality as the " Cow Ford," is correct.

"Breadth rather more than three-tenths of an inch. Inhabits the North-West Territory."

The annexed is a fac-simile of Say's figures. I cannot acquiesce in Dr. Binney's opinion that *H. porcina* Say "appears to correspond to *H. hirsuta* Say in an immature state."

Say originally described *H. hirsuta* in Nicholson's Encyclopædia (1816), the description was also published in the Journal of the Academy in 1817. In the same Journal (1821), he enumerates it, among other species observed in the Western regions, as being "common as far as Council Bluff."

It seems to me in the highest degree improbable that Say would fall into such an error as to describe a young *hirsuta* not only as an adult shell, but even as a different species.

Unfortunately no authentic specimen is now in existence, and no record of the examination of one by any of Say's contempo raries. Dr. Binney does not refer to the species in the Boston Journal, and in the Terr. Moll. only in the few words above quoted. De Kay and Pfeiffer merely copy Say's description.

That Say's figures accurately portray the species, may be inferred from the correctness of those of the other shells represented on the same plate. The outline figure, showing the natural size, exhibits an aperture by no means agreeing with that of an immature *hirsuta*, having rather more than four whorls.

Say describes the epidermis of *H. porcina* as *rugose*, with minute, very numerous *bristles*. The epidermis of *hirsuta* and *fraterna* is not mentioned, but the one species is said to be "covered with short, numerous, rigid *hairs*," and the other to be "minutely hirsute." In his description of *H. palliata*, say uses the expression "epidermis fuscous, rugose, with very numerous minute tuberculous acute prominences;" he was unacquainted with the character of the epidermis of *H. inflecta* when he published its description. In his remarks on that species he says, "several specimens were found, but all dead shells, and destitute of their epidermis." If Say's types of *H. porcina* were young shells, they were surely rather of *H. inflecta* than of *hirsuta*. I have specimens of the former from Michigan, sent to me by Professor Winchell, and from Georgia by Bishop Elliott, which, as regards the epidermis, lead to that conclusion.

I anticipate, however, that further researches will prove this to be a distinct species. The publication here of Say's description and figures will surely induce inquiry.

Helix pustula Fer.

FIG. 1, p. 42.

SYNONYMY.

Helix *pustula Fer.* Desh. in Fer. Hist. I. p. 78. No. 102, t. 50. fig. 1.
—— " *Pfr.* Mon. I. p. 422. No. 1096, 1848.
—— " *Chem.* ed. II. Helix. No. 389, p. 376, t. 65, fig. 18–20 ?
—— " *Rv.* Conch. Icon. No. 721, pl. 121, 1852.
—— *leporina W. G. Binney*, Notes on N. Amer. Land Shells, Proc.
Acad. Phil. p. 191, ex parte. 1857.
(non Binney in Terr. Moll.)

The following is a copy of the description by Deshayes,—

" H. PUSTULA.

" T. orbiculato-depressâ, tenue striatâ, anguste umbilicatâ; umbilico obtuso; rufâ vel pallide corneâ; anfr. angustis, convexiusculis, suturâ depressâ conjunctis, ultimo basi convexiore prope aperturam deflexo, coarctato; aperturâ angustâ, arcuatâ, obliquâ, albâ; marginibus reflexis, basi dente mediocri, linguiformi, conjunctis; labro bidentato, dentibus approximatis inæqualibus.

" Habite le Texas (Say) (Coll. Ferussac)."

In the description in French, the shell is said to have 4½ whorls, and to be 4 or 5 mill. in diam. As to the umbilicus, I extract the following passage :—

"Le dernier tour est convex en dessous ; un ombilic étroit est ouvert à son centre, et cet ombilic est en partie caché par l'extrémité du bord droit qui s'implante et se dilate sur son pourtour."

Pfeiffer in Mon. I. describes this species as "*suboblecte perforata*," and gives as measurements—"diam. maj. 6, min. 5½, alt. 3 mill." In Mon. III. he has the following, as variety of *H. pustula,*—

β. *pilosa*, umbilico fere omnino obtecto. (Mus. Cuming. spec. authent.)
H. leporina Gould in Proc. Bost. Soc. 1848, p. 39.
"   "   *Reeve* Conch. Ic. No. 722, t. 121.

I suspect that Pfeiffer's description in vol. I. rather refers to *H. leporina.* In Vol. III. Pfeiffer suggests that *H. Lecontii* Lea may be an umbilicate variety of *H. pustula,*—it is identical with *H. loricata* Gould.

The magnified figure (fig. 20) in Chem. ed. 2, is quite unintelligible.

Dr. Binney in Terr. Moll. describes as *H. pustula* Fer. a shell which I believe to be entirely distinct. He says of it,—" the spire is flat, has five closely revolving, rounded whorls, separated by a deep suture, the outermost obtusely angular at its upper limit; beneath convexly rounded into a large umbilicus, one-third the breadth of the base, and exhibiting the other whorls within, and with a constriction behind the lip." He mentions that it is found at Darien, and Lee county, Georgia, and in Florida. In his "Remarks" Dr. Binney speaks of the umbilical perforation as being "far broader than in any other of the polygyral group."

Comparing the two descriptions above quoted, I was for some time at a loss to understand Dr. Binney's species.

In the early part of the present year I received, through the kindness of Dr. Wilson of Darien, Ga., several specimens which I found to be the *H. pustula* Binney. This led me more carefully to examine a number of hirsute shells, collected by Bishop Elliott, Mr. Postell, and Mr. Dorman, which were labelled in the cabinets both of Mr. W. G. Binney and myself, *H. leporina* Gould. I am now satisfied that they are *H. pustula* Fer., distinct from *H. leporina*, and that Dr. Wilson's Darien shell, the *H. pustula* Binney, is an undescribed species.

The groove within the umbilicus, is a very marked feature in Ferussac's species (see fig. 1, p. 42), and though not referred to in the description is distinctly shown in one of his figures; it is entirely wanting in *H. leporina*, and also in the Darien shell (fig. 2, p. 42). This groove is not only an external character, but its presence modifies the internal structure of the shell. On opening the base of the last whorl immediately behind the aperture, a strongly developed transverse tubercle is seen within, from which a strong ridge-like lamella runs round the umbilical opening, corresponding in extent with the groove. This tubercle, and the extension of it, are entirely disconnected by a sinus or channel from the floor of the penult whorl.

The hirsute character of this species is not alluded to by any author. The outer edge of the peristome in specimens from St. Augustine, is of a deep rose color.

In his "Notes on American Land Shells," Proc. Acad. Phil. 1857, Mr. W. G. Binney gives St. Simon's Island and Savannah, Ga., as habitats of *H. leporina*. He refers to the shells above alluded to as to which we both were in error, and which we have since determined to be *H. pustula* Fer.

The measurements of a specimen of average size, are as follows:

Diam. maj. 5, min. 4, alt. 2¼, mill.

For specimens of *H. pustula* from the neighborhood of Savannah, I am indebted to Bishop Elliott, from St. Simon's

Island to Mr. Postell, and from St. Augustine, Florida, to Mr. Dorman.

Helix leporina Gould.

SYNONYMY.

Helix *leporina* Gould Proc. Bost. Soc. N. II. p. 39,	1848.
—— " *Binney* Terr. Moll. II. p. 199, pl. xl. a fig. 1,	1851.
—— " *Reeve* Conch. Icon. No. 722,	1852.
—— *pustula Pfr. var.* Mon. III. No. 1575,	1853.

The following is a copy of Dr. Gould's description:

"H. LEPORINA.

"T. parvâ, lenticulari, lucidâ, rufo-corneâ, pilosiusculâ, leviter striatâ, vix perforatâ; spirâ depressâ, anfr. 5, convexiusculis, ultimo supernò subangulato; regione umbilicali excavato; aperturâ lunatâ, labro incumbente, reflexo, roseo, dentes duos albos sinum amplectentes gerente; lamellâ columellari obliquâ, albâ, erectâ, acutâ, rectangulari, callo lineari supernè ad angulum aperturæ junctâ. Diam. ½, alt. ⅛ poll. Hab. Mississippi and Arkansas.

"Intermediate between *H. hirsuta* and *H. inflecta*, though smaller than either. It is less globose than *hirsuta*, while the aperture is much the same, except that the sinus of the lip is formed by the projection of two teeth instead of by an emargination, in this respect resembling *H. inflecta*. From the latter it differs in the columellar tooth. It resembles *H. pustula* still more, but the umbilical region wants the peculiar channel of that species."

Pfeiffer states, in his before-mentioned letter to Mr. W. G. Binney, that he now thinks this species distinct from *H. pustula* Fer.

Reeve remarks,—"It has been much doubted whether this and *H. pustula* are not varieties of the same, still the smaller shell has the larger umbilicus." He gives as habitat, Tennessee.

H. leporina is larger than *H. pustula*, less elevated, the

whorls are less convex, the incremental striæ less numerous and
distinct, and the aperture is wider. The umbilicus is more
nearly covered by the lip, and is without the groove which
prevails in Ferussac's species.

Within and near the aperture, there is what may be called
the "*fulcrum*," extending from the floor of the last to that of
the penultimate whorl, and approaching in character to, but less
strongly developed, than that in *H. monodon* Rack. The outer
edge of this *fulcrum* is uneven,—in one of my specimens somewhat denticulated.

The measurements of a rather large example are,—

Diam. maj. 6, min. 5, alt. 2½ mill.

In my cabinet is a specimen from Green Co., Indiana, received from Dr. T. R. Ingalls, one from the vicinity of Helena,
Arkansas, for which I am indebted to Mr. H. Van Nostrand,
—and one given to me by Mr. W. G. Binney, as to the habitat
of which I am uncertain. Mr. Binney has a specimen collected
in Illinois.

Helix pustuloides Bland.

Fig. 2.   Page 42.

SYNONYMY.

Helix *pustula Binney* Terr. Moll. II. p. 201, pl. xxxix. fig. 3.   1851.

T. late et perspective umbilicatâ, planorboideâ, tenuiusculâ, rufo-vel
pallide-corneâ, minute striatulâ; epidermide tenui, pilosiusculâ; spirâ
vix elevatâ; anfr. 4–4½, convexiusculis, lente accrescentibus, ultimo superne ad peripheriam obtuse angulato, ad aperturam gibboso-constricto,
subito deflexo, basi deviante; suturâ valde impressâ; umbilico lato, ½
diam. maj. æquante, omnes anfractus monstrante, præsertim penultimum;
aperturâ obliquâ, lunato-circulari; dente erecto, obliquo, albo, lamelliformi, in pariete aperturali munito, callo lineari subarcuato superne ad

angulum aperturæ juncto; perist. reflexo, roseo, marginibus conniventibus, dentibus duobus sinu disjunctis instructo.

Shell widely umbilicate, planorboid, thin, rufous or pale horn-colored, delicately striated, with thin sparingly hirsute epidermis; spire scarcely elevated; whorls 4–4½, slightly convex, gradually increasing, the last subangular at the periphery, at the aperture gibbous, constricted, suddenly deflexed, beneath devious; suture rather deeply impressed; umbilicus wide, equal to one-third of the larger diam. of the shell, showing all, but especially the penult whorl; aperture oblique, crescentic, with erect, oblique, white parietal lamelliform tooth, joined to the upper angle of the aperture by a slightly arcuate, filiform callus; peristome reflexed, with margins approaching, and having two dentiform lobes separated by a deep fissure.

Diam. maj. 5½, min. 4½, alt. 2½.

Habitat.—Near Darien, Georgia. For the specimens in my cabinet I am indebted to Dr. S. W. Wilson. As to the *station* of the species, I copy the following from one of his interesting letters:

"The place has an eastern exposure to the sea, high tides rising to the base of the low bluff where they exist. The growth of trees, which consists mostly of live oak and *Celtis occidentalis*, has never been cleared off; the *Palmetto serrulata* flourishes as an undergrowth. The soil is covered for a few inches in depth with oyster shells thrown there by the Indians, and decayed leaves and fragments of branches are of course over all these, under which, and among the superficial oyster shells, the Helices live. *H. pustula* is nowhere near, or at least a rigid search did not reveal any. *H. concava* (dead) occurs in small numbers. *H. inflecta* abundantly."

I have one dead specimen from Alabama, sent to me by Mr. Anthony.

Observations.—In my notes on *H. pustula* Fer. I have

referred to Dr. Binney's description of the shell now under consideration. *H. pustuloides* is intermediate in size between *H. pustula* and *H. leporina*—is less globose than the former, and more sparingly hirsute. It differs widely from both in the character of the umbilicus—the aperture is much like that of *pustula*, but more narrow than that of *leporina*. The inferior tooth on the peristome is more developed laterally than in *H. pustula*—indeed it has a somewhat bifid appearance, in which respect it is more allied to *H. leporina*.

The *fulcrum* in *H. pustuloides* is of the same nature as that in *H. leporina*, but less developed, and with the outer edge entire.

The accompanying figures show the base of *H. pustuloides* (fig. 2) and *H. pustula* (fig. 1).

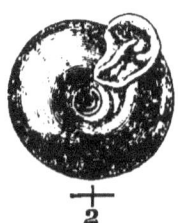

Dr. Binney's figure imperfectly represents the former, and as regards the size of the umbilicus is inconsistent with his description.

Helix glaphyra Say.

Say's description was published in Nicholson's Encyclopædia (Amer. Ed. 1816), and is as follows;—

"H. GLAPHYRA.

"Shell very much depressed, thin, fragile, pellucid, polished; whorls five, regularly rounded, and with obsolete and irregular wrinkles across them; beneath whitish; umbilicus moderate, not exhibiting the volutions. Pl. 1, fig. 3.

"Taken by Mr. G. Ord in his garden in Philadelphia.

"It considerably resembles *Helix nitens* of Europe, particularly in being whitish beneath, and will be properly arranged next that species in the systems."

Say's figure, of which the annexed is a fac-simile, is unintelligible,—it shows 3½ to 4 whorls only. He gives no measurement in his description,—the largest diameter of the figure is 9 mill.

Through the kindness of Mr. W. G. Binney I am enabled to publish the following extracts from a letter addressed in September, 1840, to his father, the late Dr. Amos Binney, by Dr. Griffith.

" *H. fuliginosa*, same as *lucubrata*, and this last name should perhaps be adopted, as I never published, except in cabinets ; it was well known by this name long before Say published, but by the laws of nomenclature he is entitled to priority. There has been some dispute as to the identity of this (*fuliginosa*), *inornata*, and what is generally considered as *glaphyra*, but I think they are distinct. *H. fuliginosa* has five whorls, dark colored, umbilicus large, lip internally white ; *inornata* is smaller, lighter colored, umbilicus partially covered, five whorls, shell not shining ; what is called *glaphyra* has five whorls, horn colored, shining, umbilicus partially covered. These three shells are closely allied, but I think distinct."

" *H. glaphyra*, the original specimen of this shell, I have often seen and studied, and always considered it as *nitens*. It was in the collection of the Academy of Sciences, but being broken was probably discarded when the Cabinet was arranged—the shell usually known as *glaphyra* is that alluded to above."

Dr. Griffith, it seems, at the date of the above letter, considered his *fuliginosa* and *H. lucubrata* Say to be identical—referred to the species now known under the name of *H. lævigata* Raf. as *H. inornata* Say, and to *H. inornata* Binney as the species usually known as *H. glaphyra*,—at the same time expressing his opinion that *H. glaphyra* Say was identical with *H. nitens*, meaning *H. cellaria*.

An amusing letter from Mr. J. G. Anthony informs me of his discovery in 1830 of many specimens of *H. cellaria*, at Providence, R. I. (a species then unknown to him), of his visit shortly afterwards to Philadelphia, and exhibition of the shells at the Academy, where they were pronounced to be *H. glaphyra* Say.

Mr. W. G. Binney, in his "Notes on American Land Shells" (Proc. Acad. Nat. Sci. Phila. 1857), considers the testimony of Dr. Griffith and Mr. Anthony conclusive as to the identity of *H. glaphyra* and *H. cellaria*, but I must confess that I am by no means satisfied on that point.

Say died in 1834. I have referred to all that can be cited as evidence of prior date.

Dr. Binney, in the Boston Journal (1840), and also in the "Terrestrial Mollusks," included *H. glaphyra* in the synonymy of *H. cellaria* Müll.

In both works he remarks: "This is the shell which was found by Mr. Say in gardens in the city of Philadelphia, and by him described as *H. glaphyra*. Its restricted habitat in cellars and gardens in the immediate vicinity of maritime cities, long since induced me to suppose it might be an imported species; and an opportunity of examining a considerable number of specimens of *H. cellaria* Müll. brought from England, enables me to say, that it is absolutely identical with that species. Shells of the same size and growth from the European and American localities cannot be distinguished from each other."

Dr. Binney, with respect to the geographical distribution of *H. cellaria*, states that it inhabits the North Eastern and Middle States, in gardens, and is common in Boston in damp cellars.

He observes that *H. inornata* Binney is often "taken to be *H. glaphyra* Say, by the Naturalists of the West, where the latter, being an introduced species (*H. cellaria* Müll.), common only near the sea shore in cellars and gardens, is not found."

Dr. Gould, in his " Report on the Invertebrata of Massachusetts" (1841), expresses the same views as Dr. Binney; he says, "there can be no doubt that the *H. glaphyra* of Say is identical with the *H. cellaria* of Müller; a comparison of shells of the same size and growth showing them to be absolutely similar in every respect."

He adds, "It seems as yet to be confined to the North Eastern and Middle States. The shell which is very commonly found marked as *H. glaphyra* is the *H. inornata* Say, in an immature state. This is a less delicate shell, but in its earlier stages, when there is but a small umbilicus, there is no inconsiderable resemblance between the two, and it would accord well with the description ; but no one familiar with the present species would ever mistake one for the other."

Dr. Binney was probably influenced by Dr. Griffith's opinion as to the identity of *H. glaphyra* and *H. cellaria*, but seems to have arrived at that conclusion rather from the assumed habitat of Say's specimen, than after critical study of his description.

Say states that the shell was taken in Mr. Ord's *garden*, but Mr. Ord has recently informed Mr. W. G. Binney that he found the single specimen, without the animal in it, on his *wharf*.

Dr. Binney, speaking of *H. cellaria*, says, "This is the shell which was found by Mr. Say in *gardens* in the city of Philadelphia, and by him described as *H. glaphyra*."

This is not only erroneous in fact, but conveys the equally erroneous impression that living specimens of *H. cellaria* were collected by Say in Philadelphia. So far as I have been able to ascertain, *H. cellaria* has never been found in that city, or even in the State of Pennsylvania; only in the New England States.

Dr. Binney and Dr. Gould, having under such circumstances pronounced Say's species to be identical with *H. cellaria*, insist on the identity of the *H. cellaria* of America and Europe. On the latter point I entirely agree with them, but the question as to *H. glaphyra* is in no way affected.

Looking at Say's description, I cannot believe that his shell, found by Mr. Ord, was *H. cellaria*. Say describes the umbilicus of *H. glaphyra* as "moderate, not exhibiting the volutions," and compares the species with *H. nitens* of Europe, "particularly in being whitish beneath." At that date *H. nitens* Gmel. and *H. nitens* Maton and Rackett were known to conchologists, the one placed by Pfeiffer in the synonymy of *H. nitida* Müll., and the other in that of *H. cellaria* Müll., both widely umbilicate, and showing the volutions to the apex, but only the latter "whitish beneath." It can scarcely be doubted that Say actually referred to *H. nitens* Mat. and Rack., noticing as a distinguishing character in *H. glaphyra*, that the volutions are not so exhibited in the umbilicus. Say describes three other species of Helix as having the umbilicus "*moderate*," viz. *septemvolva, avara,* and *tridentata*. As to the first he adds, "attenuated to the apex so as to exhibit the remaining volutions," to the second, "not exhibiting the volutions," but no further detail is given as to the umbilicus of the third species.

I know not how any one can assume that Say would have described the umbilicus of a shell identical with the European or American *cellaria*, in the language employed by him in his diagnosis of *glaphyra*. The more I study his descriptions, the more I appreciate his general acuteness and accuracy, and believe that full justice has not been done to his labors.

Say described *H. ligera* in 1821 as having the "umbilicus very small," and remarked that it "approaches nearest to *H. glaphyra*, but is readily distinguished by the greater convexity of the spire, and the *smaller* umbilicus."

This is relied upon as supporting the opinion that *glaphyra* and *cellaria* are identical, or at least that the former and *inornata* Binney are not so.

H. inornata Say (1822), which is I consider *H. lævigata*

Raf. (Fer.), is said to have the "umbilicus small, profound," and the species is described as having (irrespective of the umbilicus), "a strong resemblance to *H. ligera.*" Now I must remark, that the umbilicus of *H. glaphyra* and *H. avara* are described by Say in the same language, which would equally well apply to that of *H. inornata* Binney, and further, that the umbilicus of *H. ligera* is not only generally smaller than that of *H. inornata* Binney, but is also less open, as the columellar termination of the peristome is partially reflected over, and curved around the perforation.

The umbilicus of *H. inornata* Say (*H. lævigata*) is larger than that of *H. inornata* Binney, and the reflection of the peristome is much like that of *H. ligera.*

European authors can only have formed their judgment on the questions regarding *H. glaphyra* from Say's writings, or those of other American conchologists, or from specimens labelled by them. Pfeiffer* describes a dark colored variety of *H. inornata* Binney under the name of *glaphyra*, as he admits in a late letter to Mr. W. G. Binney.

Reeve's description and figure are also of *H. inornata* Binney.

Deshayes† (Fer. Hist.) has *glaphyra* in the synonymy of *cellaria*, evidently relying on the opinions of Gould and Binney.

The North American shell which agrees most closely with Say's *glaphyra* is *H. inornata* Binney,—it occurs in Pennsylvania, must have been known to Say, and there is abundant evidence to show that many conchologists so interpreted it.

When I visited the Academy at Philadelphia in October, 1857, I found in the cabinet a specimen of *H. inornata* Binney labelled *H. glaphyra* Say, in the handwriting, as I was informed, of Mr. J. Phillips. Mr. W. G. Binney then explained to me,

---

* Pfeiffer (Mon. I. p. 112) suggests that *H. subplana* is the same as his *glaphyra*, but the species are most certainly distinct.

† Deshayes, in his remarks on *H. dissidens* (Fer. His. I. p. 97), conjectures that American conchologists have confounded that species with the *H. cellaria* of Europe. It seems to be rather a variety of *H. concava* Say.

that many years ago Mr. Phillips had charge of the cabinet, and so labelled the specimen referred to, but had since admitted his determination to be erroneous.

With respect to *H. inornata* Say, described as "subglobose," and having "a strong resemblance to *H. ligera*," I cannot acquiesce in the opinion that it has been correctly identified by Dr. Binney. I have already stated my belief that Say's *inornata* is the *H. lævigata* Raf., the species confounded by Dr. B. with *H. lucubrata* Say. On a future occasion I propose to examine these questions more fully, but desire now to place on record the following interesting points relating to them.

When Dr. Binney was in Paris, he examined the shells in the Museum at the Jardin des Plantes, and among his notes made at the time, and now in the possession of his son, is the following,—"*H. inornata* Say is represented by the shell which I have figured as *H. lucubrata* Say.*"*

Say knew and had a specimen of *H. lævigata*. In the cabinet of Mr. Poulson, at Philadelphia, there is a specimen, as Mr. W. G. Binney informs me, labelled in Say's handwriting "Helix,—Claiborne, Ala."

In 1857, I saw at the Academy specimens of *H. lævigata*, labelled by Phillips, *H. inornata* Say.

For the present I leave *H. glaphyra* Say in the catalogue of North American Helices, as one which cannot be identified with absolute certainty, but under a strong impression that it is identical with *H. inornata* Binney.

It may be said that the question discussed at so much length is of little real importance, but if by showing how Say's species have been misunderstood, I promote a more careful study of his writings, I at least shall be satisfied.

Helix albolabris Say.

SYNONYMY.

Helix *albolabris* *Say* Nich. Encyc. (Amer. Ed.) IV. p. 181, pl. 1, fig. 1.
    1816.
—— " " Amer. Conch. No. 2, pl. 13,   1831.
——. " *Binney* Bost. Jl. I. p. 475, pl. 13,   1837.
—— *major* " " " 473, " 12,   "
—— *albolabris* *Chemn.* ed. 2, Helix, p. 81, pl. 15, fig. 7, 8.
—— " *Desh.* in Fer. Hist. p. 137, pl. 43, fig. 1–5, pl. 46 A, fig. 7.
—— " *Pfr.* Mon. I. No. 757,   1848.
—— *major* *Binney* Terr. Moll. II. p. 96, pl. 1,   1851.
—— *albolabris* " " " " 99, pl. 2,   "
—— " *Reeve* Conch. Icon. fig. 624, 656,   1852.
—— " *W. G. Binney* Reprint of Say, p. 5, 33,   1857.

Say thus describes this species in Nicholson's Encyclopædia,—

"H. ALBOLABRIS.

"Shell thin, fragile, convex, imperforated; with six volutions, whorls obtusely wrinkled across, and spirally striated with very fine impressed lines, a little waved by passing over the wrinkles, both becoming extinct towards the apex, which is perfectly smooth; aperture lunated, not angulated at the base of the column, but obtusely curved, lip contracting the mouth abruptly, widely reflected, flat and white.

"Length of the column three-fifths of an inch; breadth one inch."

The form of the shell referred to by Say has been confounded by European authors with *H. exoleta* Binney (*H. zaleta* Say), from which, however, it is entirely distinct. Dr. Leidy, from whom I sought information on the subject, wrote to me in 1857 as follows: "There is no doubt, I think, that *H. albolabris* and *H. exoleta* are distinct species, as their internal anatomy is quite different." This effectually disposes of the hypothesis of Deshayes, who, writing of the latter species (Fer. Hist.), remarks,—"Il est à présumer que l' examen de l' animal donnera la preuve qu'il est identiquement semblable à celui de l' *albola-bris.*" I may add that figs. 19, 20, pl. 10, in Chem. ed. 2. Helix, and fig. 6, pl. 46 A, in Fer. Hist., are of *H. exoleta,* which is erroneously placed in the synonymy of *H. albolabris.*

It will be seen that I do not concur with Dr. Binney in separating *H. major* from *H. albolabris.* Dr. Binney writes (1837), in the Boston Journal,—"Mr. Conrad informs me that he obtained this shell (*H. major*) several years since, in Alabama, and considered it a new species, but was deterred from publishing it as such, by the generally received opinion that it was only a variety of *H. albolabris.*" He observes also,—"this was probably Mr. Say's view, as the specimens figured by Ferussac were received from him."

In the "Terrestrial Mollusks," Dr. Binney thus remarks on *H. major :—*

"It cannot be confounded with any other than *H. albolabris,* and differs from it in the following particulars :—It is much more globose, of a coarser and more solid texture, and the striæ of increase are much more raised and prominent, so much so, indeed, as to leave distinct grooves between them. The revolving striæ, so distinct on that shell, are either wanting or very indistinct. The aperture is smaller in proportion to the size of the shell, less flattened towards the plane of the base, and more rounded. The pillar lip and umbilicus are in many instances covered with a smooth and shining, semi-transparent, testaceous callus. The margin of the lip is thickened, the lip itself is narrower, less abruptly reflected, and not so much flattened, and there is often a tooth-like process on the inner and upper side of the margin near the umbilicus. The color of the epidermis is generally much darker. The only considerable variation in the characters of the shell is caused by the depression of the spire in some individuals, and indeed in all specimens from certain localities. In its most perfect condition it is often subconical. It is subject to some irregularities in the form of the mouth, and there is sometimes an indication of pale bands in the epidermis of the body whorl."

He adds,—

"That this is not the same species increased in size by the influence of a warmer climate, would seem to be proved by the fact that other species are not larger in Florida than in situations further north, and that *H. tridentata* Say, common in every part of the country, is smaller in Florida than elsewhere. The color of the respective animals is widely different."

Dr. Binney's illustration as to the influence of climate is an unfortunate one. In the Boston Journal he makes the same remark, mentioning, however, *H. fallax*, instead of *H. tridentata*, and with his notes on the latter (which he erroneously treats as identical with the former), he figures (pl. 18, fig. 2) as "the small variety from Florida" of *tridentata*, a distinct southern species, which never attains a much larger size, viz. the *H. Hopetonensis* of Shuttleworth, who, in its synonymy, refers to that same figure.

With respect to the larger size of *H. major*, it may be observed that species in this, as well as other countries, attain extraordinary development in some particular district—if size alone be considered, there is quite as much reason for separating the *H. tridentata* and *H. alternata* of Ohio from the forms prevailing in the Eastern States, as *H. major* from *H. albolabris*.

The differences in sculpture from certain localities are also very striking. On Long Island, and near Albany, N. Y., there is a small, depressed, almost smooth variety of *H. alternata*,—the Ohio form is striated, while the southern varieties are strongly ribbed. The Ohio *H. tridentata* is almost smooth,—I have examples from Pennsylvania with well-defined, distinct ribs. Some forms of *H. appressa* are without, while others have very numerous fine revolving striæ. Dr. Binney is certainly in error as to the absence or indistinctness of such striæ in *H. major*. They exist in all the individuals of my extensive suite of specimens, including the forms of which he gives figures.

The tooth-like process on the margin of the lip near the umbilicus is by no means a good specific character; it exists in *H. thyroidus* from Georgia and Tennessee, and in *H. exoleta* Binney from Columbus, Ohio; indeed it is shown in the figure of the latter in Terr. Moll. pl. 10. I have noticed it moderately developed in specimens of *H. albolabris* from Ohio and Massachusetts.

I learn from Dr. Leidy that he has not examined the animal of *H. major*. *H. major* and *H. albolabris* are in fact subject to much variation in size, color, texture, sculpture, form of aperture, and lip, and development of the latter, but there are no constant characters in either to justify their separation as distinct species. In my cabinet are specimens which I refer to *H. major*, from Florida, Georgia, Tennessee, and South Carolina, forms which seem to be intermediate from Alabama, Missouri, and Wisconsin,—and of *H. albolabris* from most of the Eastern, Middle, and Western States, as well as from Virginia, North Carolina, and Canada West.

The following are measurements of varieties of *H. major*,—

Diam. maj. 35, min. 30, Alt. 23, mill. (*globose*), Florida.
   "   "   37, "   32, "   22, "   "   Georgia.
   "   "   45, "   36, "   22, "   (*depressed*), "
   "   "   38, "   32, "   18, "   (*flattened*), "
   "   "   31, "   26, "   18, "   (*elevated*), "
   "   "   32, "   28, "   16, "   (*depressed*), Wisconsin.
   "   "   24, "   20, "   12, "   "   Missouri.

The two latter I call intermediate forms—the following *H. albolabris*,—

Diam. maj. 35, min. 30, Alt. 19, mill. N. Carolina.
   "   "   32, "   26, "   15, "   Ohio.
   "   "   28, "   24, "   15, "   Canada West.
   "   "   26, "   21, "   12, "   Pennsylvania.
   "   "   23, "   19, "   11, "   Tennessee.

I possess two specimens of the above mentioned Wisconsin shell. Both have a remarkably thick and dark-colored epidermis, the tooth-like process on the lip near the umbilicus very prominently developed, and in one the spiral striæ are nearly obsolete. From its peculiar general aspect this seems even more worthy of being treated as a distinct species than the typical (globose) form of *H. major*. *H. albolabris* is frequently found with a small parietal tooth, but such shells are distinct in form from *H. exoleta*. I have specimens of *H. multilineata* with the same process.

Deshayes mentions Guadeloupe, on the authority of specimens in the Museum, as habitat, though rarely, of *H. albolabris*. I need scarcely say that in this there must be some error.

Remarks on Certain Species of North American Helicidæ.

Reprinted from the Transactions of the Lyceum of Natural History, New York, December, 1858.

BY THOMAS BLAND.

(Continued from vol. vi. p. 362.)

Read 20th December, 1858.

Helix auriculata, Say.

SYNONYMY.

Polygyra *auriculata*	*Say* Nich. Enc. Am. ed.		1816
"	"	" Jl. Acad. N. S., Phila., I. p. 277.	1818
Helix	"	*Fer.* Prod., No. 98.	1822
"	"	*Binney* Bost. Jl. III., p. 384 (ex parte) Pl. xix., fig. 1.	1840
"	"	*De Kay* N. Y. Moll., p. 47, pl. 3, fig. 28.	1843
"	"	*Pfr.* Mon. Hel. I. No. 1084, excl. var.	1848
"	"	*Chemn.* ed. II. Helix p. 371, t. 65, fig. 3, 4.	
"	"	*Desh.* in Fer. Hist. p. 76 (excl. var.) pl. 50, fig. 4.	
"	"	*Binney* Terr. Moll. II. p. 186 (ex parte), pl. xl., fig. 1 (left hand).	1851
"	"	*Reeve* Conch. Icon. No. 700. excl. fig.	1852
Polygyra,	"	*W. G. Binney*, reprint of Say, p. 10.	1856
Helix,	"	" Notes on Amer. Land Shells in Proc. Acad., Phila., p. 191.	1857
		" " 200.	1858

The following is a copy of Say's description :—

POLYGYRA AURICULATA.—Shell beneath, convex ; whorls five, a little rounded, crossed by numerous raised equidistant lines, forming grooves between them ; spire very little raised ; lateral line (extending from the outer whorl to the apex), not convex, but somewhat concave ; mouth very unequal ; lips prominent above, appressed to the preceding whorl beneath ; pillar lip suddenly reflected, and pressed into the mouth at an acute angle, beneath very acutely concave ; outer lip a little more prominent in the middle, and within the edge protruded into the mouth ; throat extremely narrow ; suture near the mouth suddenly reflected from the preceding whorl, and carinate ; umbilicus dilated, very small within, and exhibiting a groove on the outer whorl.

Breadth of the female nearly half an inch, of the male about three-tenths. Inhabits Florida. Cabinet of the Academy. This curious species we found near St. Augustine, East Florida, in a moist situation. They were observed in considerable numbers; the color is reddish brown, indistinctly banded with whitish lines, sometimes with darker ones ; mouth white.

The specimens preserved in the Cabinet of the Academy at Philadelphia, said to have been Say's, but labelled in the handwriting of Mr. Philipps, agree with those collected by Mr. O. M. Dorman, and to which I refer in these notes.

The group to which this species belongs has been very much misunderstood. In 1816 Say described *H. auriculata* and *H. avara*,—he sent specimens to Ferussac, who enumerated them in his Prodromus, and published figures in advance of the text of the Hist. des Moll., which Deshayes contributed many years later.

Dr. Binney erroneously considered *H. avara* to be the immature form of *auriculata*, and indeed referred all the forms known to him to the latter species. In 1852 Shuttleworth described Helix *uvulifera*, and Reeve published the same, with a figure, as H. *florulifera.* Of this I received specimens from Shuttleworth in 1853,—it appeared to be unknown to American conchologists. Subsequently I had a shell from Dr. Budd, without name or locality, but unquestionably the *H. avara* Say, though by no means agreeing with any species so labelled in the cabinets to which I had access, including that of Dr. Binney, in the possession of Mr. W. G. Binney.

During 1858 I received, through the kindness of Mr. O. M. Dorman, a number of *H. auriculata*, collected by himself at

St. Augustine, and several of the rare *H. avara* from the vicinity of the river St. John, East Florida. After careful examination of the whole subject, I am of opinion that *H. auriculata* Say, and *avara* Say, are entirely distinct,—that the forms referred to by Dr. Binney as *avara*, and by him, Pfeiffer, and Deshayes, as varieties of *auriculata*, are likewise distinct, and that the comparatively small shell commonly labelled *H. auriculata* in our cabinets, but generally without authentic habitat, is a variety of *H. uvulifera* Shuttl.

Pfeiffer in Mon. I. refers to Ferussac's figure 3 (pl. 50), as var. *minor* of *H. auriculata*, but with doubt in Mon. III. to the same, in the synonymy of *H. uvulifera* Shuttl.

Reeve's fig. 700 (pl. 119), referred to by Pfeiffer as *auriculata*, appears to be of the same form.

Deshayes gives an elaborate description in French of this species; alluding to the variety, he says : " La variété est plus petite, plus mince, plus transparente ; mais ces caractères dépendent probablement de l'âge. Il en est sans doute de même relativement aux différences dans les formes et les proportions de l'ouverture." He derived and adopted, I presume, that opinion from the Boston Journal.

To aid in identifying this and the allied species, I give the annexed figure I. of the aperture of *H. auricu-* Fig. I. *lata* Say, double the natural size, taken from a living specimen collected by Mr. O. M. Dorman at St. Augustine.

H. auriculata Say.

H. auriculata may be distinguished by its larger size, the greater development of the several parts of its curious aperture, and especially by the sudden outward deflexure of the central part of the labrum, which has a deep scrobiculation behind it, corresponding with the upper tooth within the aperture. The portion of the labium extending from the inferior angle of the parietal intruded tooth is erect, and more elevated than in any other of the species.

The following are the measurements of the largest and smallest specimens, selected from about thirty of those collected by Mr. Dorman:—

Diam. maj. 16, min. 13, Alt. 7½ mill.
"   "   12,   "   10½, " 6   "

I have no authentic information of the occurrence of this species in any other locality than at St. Augustine, and its immediate neighbourhood, and no other form was there found by Mr. Dorman.

It is difficult to understand Say's observation as to the different size of the male and female, referring, as he evidently does, to the shell, and not to the animal. His measurements correspond with those of the smaller diameters of my specimens. No example with the indistinct bands mentioned by Say has come under my notice.

No *fulcrum* or tubercle exists in any member of this group. The groove in the last whorl, exhibited in the umbilical region, has a corresponding somewhat convex surface in the interior.

I would explain that the forms figured as *auriculata* by Binney in Terr. Moll., pl. xl., fig. 1 (right hand), by Ferussac, pl. 50, fig. 3, and by Reeve in Conch. Icon., pl. cxix., No. 700, appear to represent the same species,—one which I consider distinct, and propose to describe as *H. auriformis.*

Binney's fig. 2 in both his works, and Reeve's pl. cxxi., No. 720, may be of a different shell, but cannot in fact be very readily made out,—the figs.1, 2 in Chemn., pl. 55, are quite unintelligible ; certainly none of them are of *H. avara* Say. To another distinct species from Georgia, confounded with *H. avara,* I give the specific name *Postelliana.*

Helix avara, Say.

Synonymy.

Polygyra *avara*	*Say* Nich. Enc. Am. ed.		1816
"	"	" Jl. Acad. N. S. Phil. I. p. 277.	1818
Helix	"	*Fer.* Prod., No. 97.	1822
"	"	*Pfr. var. β. minor,* Mon. Hel. I., No. 1087 (ex parte).	1848
"	"	*Desh.* in Fer. Hist., p. 78, pl. 50, fig. 2.	
"	"	*Chemn.* ed. II., Helix, p. 370 (ex parte), excl. fig.	
"	"	*Reeve* Conch. Icon. (ex parte), No. 720, excl. fig.	1852
Polygyra	"	*W. G. Binney* reprint of Say, p. 11.	1856
"	"	" Notes on Amer. Land Shells in Proc. Acad. Phila., p. 200.	1858

Say's description is as follows:—

P. AVARA.—" Shell covered with numerous short, robust hairs ; spire convex ; whorls four, regularly rounded, with hardly elevated lines forming grooves, which are much more conspicuous near the mouth ; mouth subreniform, two projecting, obtuse teeth on the outer lip within, separated by a deep sinus ; outer lip elevated, equal, describing two-thirds of a circle ; pillar lip elevated, broadly but not profoundly emarginate, concave beneath, and connected to the inner side by an elongated, lamelliform tooth, which is placed obliquely on the penultimate whorl near the middle of the mouth ; lips almost equally prominent, continued ; umbilicus moderate, not exhibiting the volutions, no groove on the ultimate whorl within it. Breadth quarter of an inch. Inhabits Florida. Cabinet of the Academy. Animal longer than the breadth of the shell, acute behind, above granulated and blackish, beneath, and each side, white.

" This we found in the orange groves of Mr. Fatio, on the River St. John, East Florida ; it is usually covered with a black, earthy coat, which is probably retained and collected by the hairs. When unencumbered by this vesture, the shell is of a horn color. It is by no means so common as the preceding species (P. auriculata)."

No specimen of this comparatively rare shell is now to be found in the cabinet of the Academy at Philadelphia.

In the above synonymy I exclude all mention of the writings of Dr. Binney, in the confident belief that he entirely misinterpreted this species. In the Boston Journal he refers to Pl. xix. fig. 1, as the mature *H. auriculata*, and to fig. 2 "as the young shell described by Say as *P. avara.*" His remarks are repeated in the Terr. Moll., with an additional observation as to the size of the shells. From the latter work I quote the following:—

"At different periods of growth the aperture differs very much in appearance, and has led naturalists into error. When the lip is just beginning to be formed, and as yet projects but little, there are two projecting teeth on its inner edge, with a deep sulcus between them; as these continue to grow, they assume more and more the appearance of lamellar folds, the lower one of which, when viewed on a line perpendicular to the base of the shell, hides the other. The columellar fold, at the same early period, appears more like an independent tooth, to each extremity of which the lip is connected. It is this variety which Mr. Say described as a distinct species, under the name of *Polygyra avara*. This opinion I derive, not so much from his descriptions as from the examination of original specimens collected and labelled by him, now in my possession. I have specimens of the mature shell smaller than any specimen of *H. avara* that I have seen, and have other specimens of *H. avara*, so called, as large as the most mature *H. auriculata*. Plate XL. fig. 1, represents the mature shell, fig. 2, the young shell, described by Say as *P. avara.*"

The whole tenor of the above remarks is certainly erroneous. With respect to the shells " collected and labelled" by Say, it is possible that he, at a period subsequent to the publication of his diagnosis, may have distributed as *H. avara* specimens similar to those figured by Dr. Binney, considering them to be variety of that species; but the figures by no means agree with, and indeed I doubt whether he ever saw the rare form *described* by Say. There is no example of it in the cabinet of Dr. Binney, now in the possession of Mr. W. G. Binney. Through his kindness I have specimens from that cabinet of the *H. avara* Binney, which are not only mature shells, but entirely distinct from Say's species.

Dr. Binney's statement that he had the mature *H. auriculata* smaller than any *H. avara* he had seen, and the latter as large as the former in its mature state, is totally unintelligible. I can only interpret it by assuming that he did not know *H. avara* Say, and confounded a small variety of *H. uvulifera* Shuttl., and the two forms, both in fact mature shells, figured in the Terr. Moll., Pl. XL. figs. 1 (right hand) and 2, with *H. auriculata.*

To European authors *H. avara* seems to have been almost entirely unknown,—the figures in Reeve and in Chemnitz do not represent it; indeed the only figure which does so approximately is that of Ferussac.

I find from the first letter written to Ferussac by Say, a copy of which, without date, is now before me, in his own handwriting,* that he sent to Ferussac specimens of *P. auriculata* and *P. avara.* In the reply, dated Paris, 15th July, 1820, are the following notes:—

"14. *P. auriculata*, precieuse espèce que je n'avais pas, nouvelle."

"15. *P. avara*, celle-ci est presque aussi curieuse, nouvelle pour moi."

Deshayes (Fer. Hist. I. p. 78) writes as to *H. avara*, referring to Ferussac's figure, Pl. 50, fig. 2:—"Avant d'avoir vu cette

---

* I am indebted to Mrs. Say for an opportunity of examining much of the correspondence of Mr. Say with Baron Ferussac and others, and would acknowledge gratefully the interest which she manifests in my endeavors to identify the species described by Mr. Say.

espèce dans la Collection de M. de Ferussac, nous l'avions prise pour une variété de l'*H. auriculata*. Après l'avoir comparée à cette dernière, nous lui avons reconnu des caractères constants, ce qui nous a determiné à la conserver comme espèce distincte."

The annexed figure II. of *H. avara* Say, double the natural

Fig. II.   size, is from a specimen collected on the St. John's

H. avara Say.

River, Florida, by Mr. O. M. Dorman. The *striæ* are incorrectly represented,—they should have been shown only at the termination of the last whorl, over a small space immediately behind the peristome.

H. avara Say may be readily distinguished by its smaller size, more delicate texture, and less globose form,—it has from 4 to 4½ whorls, and is the only species of the group which is hirsute. The superior tooth on the labrum is armed with a hook as in the other species, but is narrower, less deeply seated, and more erect; the inferior one is rather a distinct tooth than a lamellar fold. The parietal process differs entirely from that of *H. auriculata*, as plainly shown in my figure. *H. avara* is without the groove on the last whorl which prevails in *auriculata*, and the forms represented by Dr. Binney as varieties of it.

The size appears to be constant,—the following are the measurements of the specimen figured :—

Diam. maj. 7, min. 6, Alt. 3 mill.

Mr. W. G. Binney (Proc. Phila. Acad., 1857, p. 191), when commenting on the figures of *H. auriculata* in the Terr. Moll., says: "I do not consider fig. 2, *H. avara* Say, as a variety of this, but a distinct species. There are some varieties of *auriculata* which may be confounded with it, but it is certainly a good species." I entirely agree in the opinion that fig. 2 represents a good species, but by no means that it is the *H. avara* Say. Mr. Binney mentions having received fine fresh hirsute specimens from Mr. Postell,—in this there must be some mistake. The *H. avara* W. G. Binney from St. Simon's Island and other parts of Georgia, is not hirsute, as Mr. Postell himself assures me, and *H. avara* Say has not been found there.

Helix uvulifera Shuttleworth.

SYNONYMY.

Helix *uvulifera Shuttleworth* Bern. Mittheil., p. 199, August.   1852
"   "   "   Diag. n. Moll., No. 2, p. 19.
"   *florulifera Reeve* Conch. Icon., No. 699, p. 119.   1852
"   *uvulifera Chemn.* Ed. II. Helix, No. 979, t. 148, fig.
           19, 20, fide Pfr.
"   "   *W. G. Binney* Notes on Amer. Land Shells,
           Proc. Phila. Acad., p. 205.   1858

Shuttleworth thus describes this species :—

" HELIX UVULIFERA.—T. rimato-perforata, superne planiuscula, subtus inflata, striata, cinereo-albida, solidula, nitidula ; anfr. 5, lente accrescentes, angusti, ultimus ad aperturam subito deflexus, subtus devius, scrobiculato-constrictus ; apertura valde obliqua, auriformis, ringens, valde coarctata ; perist. acutum, reflexo-patulum, marginibus plica linguiformi oblonga medio excavata profunde intrante junctis, dextro lamella profunde immersa in apicula filiformi reflexa desinente, basali tuberculo dentiformi obliquo et sinuoso instructo.

" Diam. maj. 12, min. 11, Alt. 7 mill.

" *Hab.*—In insulis parvis ' Long Keys ' sinu dicto ' Sarazota,' Florida Austr. (Rugel).

" *Obs.*—Specimina numerosissima examinavi.   Proxime H. auriculatæ affinis, sed textura, colore, ac apertura minus coarctata, peristomateque minus producto satis distincta.   H. Ariadnæ Pfr. in Chemn., ed. 2, tab. 65, f. 29–31, etiam affinis, at differt figura testa tantum rimata sine vestigio perforationis.   Nomen specificum ab apicula lamella marginis dextri peristomatis, Uvulæ Humanæ haud dissimili, assumptum. Sed character hic in omnibus speciebus affinibus plus minusve obvius est."

The annexed figure III. of the aperture of *H. uvulifera* Shuttl., twice the natural size, is from a specimen received direct from the author of the species.

FIG. III.

H. uvulifera may be distinguished from *H. auriculata* by the character of the labrum, which is equally produced from the superior angle of the parietal process, to the base of the inferior tooth

H. uvulifera Shuttl.

or fold, where it is reflected, sometimes appressed to the last whorl. The lower angle of the parietal process is connected with the inner termination of the labrum by a flat, more or less developed callus. The umbilical region is less open, and there is no groove within it on the last whorl.

This species is variable in size, texture, and sculpture. Mr. Shuttleworth's specimen is opaque, of the color indicated in his description,—irregularly, and, compared with *H. auriculata*, slightly striated.

I have one example of large size, from the cabinet of the late Mr. Samuel Lounsbury, which is white, translucent, and almost smooth,—the habitat unknown.

Of the more common form, usually labelled *H. auriculata* in American cabinets, I received very many specimens from Mr. Anthony and other correspondents, but without any note of the locality in which they were collected. For one from Corpus Christi, Texas, I am indebted to Mr. W. G. Binney. This variety is of a yellowish horn color, shining, strongly striated above and at the base, and generally smaller than the shel described by Shuttleworth.

I add the measurements of the specimens referred to :—

Diam. maj. 11½, min. 10, Alt. 6 mill, whorls 5, Shuttleworth.
"   "   14   "   12 " 7 "   " 6, Lounsbury.
"   "   9   "   8 " 5½ "   " 5½, W. G. Binney.

Helix Postelliana Bland.

T. rimato-perforatâ, superne convexiusculâ, costulato-striatâ, subtus inflato-convexâ, læviusculâ; fusco-corneâ, tenui, nitidâ, subpellucidâ; spirâ vix elevatâ; anfr. 5, lente accrescentibus, convexiusculis, ultimo ad aperturam deflexo, disjuncto, scrobiculato-constricto ; suturâ impressâ ; aperturâ albâ, obliquâ, auriformi, coarctatâ; perist. acuto, continuo, marginibus plicâ linguiformi, oblongâ, intrante, superne excavatâ, junctis ; dextro lamellâ uncatâ profunde immersâ, basali dente lamelliformi, erecto, vix obliquo, intra aperturam producto et recurvato, instructo.

Shell perforate, above slightly convex, with rib-like striæ wider apart and more prominent behind the aperture; beneath inflated, convex, almost smooth, and with microscopic spiral lines; brown horn color, thin, shining, subpellucid; whorls 5, gradually increasing, rather convex, the last deflected and turned outwards from the preceding one, scrobiculate, constricted, grooved within the umbilical region; suture impressed; aperture white, oblique, ear-shaped, contracted; peristome acute, continuous, the margins joined by a tongue-shaped fold, excavated above, entering into the aperture, the right margin having a deeply-seated lamella, which terminates in a reflexed hook, the base with an erect lamelliform, scarcely oblique tooth, produced into, and recurved within the aperture. Diam. maj. 9½; min. 8½, mill. Alt. 5 mill.

Habitat.—Wayne Co., Ware Co. and St. Simon's Island, Ga., Postell!: Camden Co., Ga., Bishop Elliott!: Glynn Co., Ga. Wilson!

Station.—Mr. Postell writes as to the Wayne Co. specimens, of which he sent me about a dozen.

" These shells are found upon the slopes of the hills, near the base, where the earth is always moist, under fallen pines, and in most cases between the bark and trunk of the trees. The animals feed, I think, on the decayed bark, and not on living vegetable matter."

The single specimen in my cabinet from Ware Co. Ga., is somewhat larger than the others—has 5½ whorls,—the aperture is brown in color, and the striæ are more conspicuous at the base.

Its measurements are,

Diam. maj. 10 ; min. 9. Alt. 5½ mill.

Observations.—This species, of which the annexed fig. IV. shows the aperture, double the natural size, is certainly distinct from the three already considered. It is smaller than

Fig. IV.

II. postelliana Bland.

H. auriculata, and the rib-like striæ, which cover the whole of that shell, are scarcely developed at the base. The form of the parietal process is very like that of *H. uvulifera*, but the continuation of its inferior angle to the inner termination of the labrum is not prostrate as in that species, but erect as in *H. auriculata*. The position and form of the upper tooth on the labrum is much the same as in that species, and in *H. uvulifera*, but the lower one is entirely different. In those it is an oblique, strongly developed, convex, sinuous fold on the margin of the labrum, not descending into the aperture, there being within a slight thickening only, corresponding with the lower exterior apertural depression.

In *H. Postelliana* there is at the base of the labrum a thin, erect, oblong, lamelliform tooth, rather oblique, but more closely marginal than the fold in the other species. The exterior of this tooth is convex, within concave, it is 1 mill. in height, and 1½ in length, and descends rapidly into the aperture, where it is recurved, and terminates obtusely opposite to the lower end of the superior tooth, there being a very distinct and tortuous sinus between the two. I have opened specimens from different localities, and find these characters constant.

This is, I believe, the shell which Dr. Binney supposed to be the *H. avara* Say—specimens from his cabinet, as well as one sent to me by the late Judge Tappan, all so labelled, induce this opinion. The small figures, however, in the Boston Journal, and Terr. Moll. scarcely represent this form.

I name this species after my liberal correspondent Mr. James Postell, in acknowledgment of the valuable assistance which I have received from him, in my endeavor to elucidate the North American Helices.

Helix auriformis Bland.

Helix *auriculata Binney*, Bost. Jl. (ex parte), pl. xix. fig. 2,   1840
"   "   *Desh.* in Fer. Hist. var. *minor*, pl. 50, fig. 3.

Helix *avara Chemn.* ed. II., Helix 370 (ex parte), t. 65, fig. 1–2.
"   " *Pfr.* Mon. I., No. 1087 (ex parte),   1848
"   *auriculata Binney,* Terr. Moll. II. (ex parte,), fig. 1,
           (right hand), 2.   1851
"   *avara Reeve* Conch. Icon, No. 720, pl. 121.   1852
"   *auriculata* "   "   "   " 700, " 119.   1852

T. rimato-perforatâ, superne depressâ, costulato-striatâ, subtus inflato-convexâ, læviusculâ ; albâ vel fusco-corneâ, tenui, spirâ brevis-
simâ ; anfr. 5½–6, planiusculis, ultimo ad aperturam deflexo, breviter
disjuncto, constricto, vix scrobiculato ; aperturâ subhorizontali, auriformi, coarctatâ ; perist. acuto, continuo, marginibus plicâ linguiformi,
brevi, intrante junctis ; dextro lamellâ obtusâ, submarginali, basali tuberculo dentiformi, obliquo et sinuoso, instructo.

ᵗ Shell perforate, above depressed, with rib-like striæ, beneath
inflated, convex, almost smooth, and with microscopic spiral
lines; white, or brown horn-color, thin ; spire very short;
whorls 5½ to 6, rather flat, the last deflected, and shortly turned
outwards from the preceding whorl, constricted, scarcely scrobiculate ; aperture sub-horizontal, ear-shaped, contracted ; peristome acute, continuous, the margins joined by a short linguiform
fold, entering within the aperture ; the right margin with an
obtuse submarginal lamella, and the base with an oblique sinuous, tooth-like fold.
Diam. maj. 11½ ; min. 10. Alt. 6 mill.
"   "   9,   "   8, "   4½ "

Habitat.—The largest specimen is from Ware Co., Ga., Postell ! The smaller is one of two specimens found in a rotten
oak log, in the neighborhood of Savannah, Ga., by my young
friend, John Elliott, a son of Bishop Elliott ; in these the striæ
at the base are more prominent than in any other specimens.
The species seems to have a wider distribution than the preceding. I have specimens from Washington Co., Texas (W. G.
Binney); from Alabama (Prof. A. Winchell and J. H. Redfield)

and many, without mention of habitat, from several correspondents.

Observations.—This species, the aperture of which is represented in Fig. V., is common in American cabinets, and usually

FIG. V.

H. auriformis Bland.

labelled *H. avara*, or var. of *H. auriculata*, but it appears to me entirely distinct. It is most nearly allied to the former, but is larger, not hirsute, and has the groove in the last whorl, within the umbilical region like the latter. The parietal fold is somewhat similar to, but does not descend so far into the aperture as that of *H. Postellania*, but the teeth on the labrum are in form and position, though more developed, rather like those of *H. avara*. They are separated by the same deep sinus, but the upper one generally without the sharp reflexed hook at its termination.

The pale and white varieties are, I believe, from Alabama, —my figure is taken from one of them, the shells are heavier, and the parietal fold especially is more developed.

I have given to this species the name *auriformis*, the general form of the aperture, with its several parts, offering a more striking resemblance to the human ear than is the case with any of its allies.

Remarks on Certain Species of North American Helicidæ.

By Thomas Bland.

Read March 5, 1860. ,

Reprinted from the Annals of the Lyceum of Natural History in New York, Vol. vII., April, 1860.

Helix espiloca Ravenel.

Plate IV. fig. 1–2.

T. rimato-perforatâ, superne convexiusculâ, subtus convexâ, striatâ, rufescente-corneâ, tenui, pilis brevissimis obsitâ; spirâ vix elevatâ ; anfr. 5 convexiusculis, ultimo ad aperturam breviter deflexo, disjuncto, scrobiculato-constricto; aperturâ perobliquâ, subreniformi, coarctatâ; perist. acuto, continuo, marginibus lamellâ superne excavatâ, dentem linguiformem emittente, junctis; dextro lamellâ latâ uncatâ, basali dente lamelliformi, erecto, intra aperturam producto et recurvato, instructo.

Shell perforate, above slightly convex, beneath convex, striated, reddish-horn colored, thin, with very short hairs ; spire scarcely elevated ; whorls 5, rather convex, the last deflected and turned outwards from the preceding one, scrobiculate, constricted, grooved within the umbilical region ; aperture very oblique, subreniform, contracted ; peristome acute, continuous, the margins joined by a lamella, excavated above, and produced into a tongue-shaped tooth ; the right margin having a broad hooked lamella, and the base an erect lamelliform tooth produced into and recurved within the aperture.

Diam. maj. 9, min. 8, Alt. 4, mill.

"   "   7 " 6 " 3 " var. *minor*.

Habitat.—Sullivan's Island, South Carolina. Dr. E. Ravenel !

Observations.—This species is certainly distinct from the others of the group. In the form of the parietal process, it is intermediate between *H. Postelliana* and *H. avara*, but most like the latter; the teeth on the peristome are very similar to those in the former, but beneath it is less inflated, the umbilical region is wider, showing more of the penultimate whorl, and it is hirsute.

I am indebted for this species to Dr. Edmund Ravenel, and

adopt the name suggested by him in correspondence with Say. He informs me that many years ago he collected specimens, and thinking the shell undescribed, forwarded some to Say, with the following label, which is still in his possession, "H. avara Say? probably new, if so call it II. espiloca." Say considered them to be *avara*.*

Seeing that Say pronounced this species and *H. Postelliana* to be *avara*, I can understand the remarks of Dr. Binney quoted by me, Annals Vol. VII. p. 31, but still am under the impression that he could not have seen the shell *described* by Say as *H. avara*.

Helix introferens, nov. sp.

Plate IV. fig. 3-4.

T. umbilicatâ, depresso-globosâ, tenuiusculâ, costulato-striatâ, corneoluteâ; spirâ convexâ; anfr. 6, convexiusculis, ultimo antice vix deflexo, ad aperturam valde constricto, bierobiculato, ad peripheriam subangulato, basi convexo, intra umbilicum excavato; aperturâ obliquâ, lunari, dente linguiformi valido, flexuoso, in pariete aperturali intrante coarctatâ; perist. albo, intus calloso, reflexo, margine dextro dente obtuso introrsum flexo, basali dente lamelliformi submarginali, in medio transversim tuberculato, instructo; dente inferiori intra aperturam producto, tuberculum validum formante.

Shell umbilicate, globose, depressed, thin, with riblike striæ, yellowish horn colored; spire convex, whorls six, moderately convex, the last scarcely descending, much constricted at the aperture, with two exterior pits, subangular at the periphery, convex beneath, grooved within the umbilicus; aperture oblique, lunate, with well developed arcuate parietal tooth; peristome white, thickened within, reflected; on the right margin an obtuse inflected tooth, at the base a submarginal lamelliform tooth, with transverse tubercle in the centre; the basal lamella continued within the aperture, where it forms a strong white tubercle.

---

* See Extracts from Dr. Ravenel's letters at page 77. I am indebted to Mrs. Say for specimens of *H. Postelliana*, with label "Helix —— ? Swamps of S. Car. written by Dr. Ravenel, with the specific name "avara S" added by Say.

Diam. maj. 15, min. 13. Alt. 7, mill. spec. from Dr. Budd's cabinet.

Diam. maj. 13, min. 11, Alt. 7, mill. spec. from Gaston Co. N. Car., Wheatley.

Var. minor. anfr 5.

Diam. maj. 11, min. 9, Alt. 6, mill. spec. from Salem, N. Car. Hartvig!

Habitat.—Gaston Co., N. Car., Wheatley. Salem, N. Car., Hartvig!

Remarks.—This shell is closely allied to the Texan species, *H. vultuosa* Gould, and also to *H. fallax* Say. It differs from the latter in the narrower umbilicus, which only shows the penultimate whorl; in the groove in the last whorl within the umbilical opening, the character of the basal tooth, and the internal tubercle (a modification of the *fulcrum* of Lea), which does not prevail in *fallax* and its immediate allies *tridentata* and *Hopetonensis.* In *H. introferens* the upper tooth is less deeply seated and less inflected, and the basal one is broader, and more elevated than in *vultuosa*, the parietal tooth is more arcuate, being indeed subangular, but is without the indication, noticeable in Gould's species, of a callus extending from its lower termination towards the upper angle of the lip. *H. vultuosa* is even smaller than the var. *minor* of my species.

Several years ago I received four or five specimens from Dr. Budd, and noticed the tubercle within the aperture, subsequently Mr. Wheatley gave me the only one in his cabinet, and the Rev. Mr. Hartvig sent me several collected by himself at Salem, N. C., where he then resided.

Helix Christyi, nov. sp.

Plate IV. fig. 5–6.

T. imperforatâ, depressâ, solidulâ, confertim costulato-striatâ, fusco-corneâ; spirâ brevi, obtusâ; anfr. 4½ convexiusculis, ultimo ad aperturam deflexo, constricto, superne gibbo, ad peripheriam subangulato; basi convexo, in medio excavato; aperturâ depressâ, dente lamelliformi valido, obliquo, in pariete aperturali intrante coarctatâ; perist. reflexo, intus albo-calloso.

Shell imperforate, depressed, rather solid, with numerous oblique rib-like striæ, dark horn-colored; spire short, obtuse; whorls 4½, rather convex, the last descending at the aperture, slightly angular at the periphery, constricted, above gibbous; base convex, excavated in the middle; aperture depressed, with a strong oblique lamelliform parietal tooth; peristome reflected, with a white callus within.

Diam. maj. 10, min. 8, Alt. 4½, mill.

Habitat.—Mountains in Cherokee Co., N. Carolina, David Christy!

Remarks.—This shell has curious affinities with other North American species. Without a hairy epidermis, and having the rib-like striæ of the small varieties of *H. tridentata* Say, it has the form of aperture, parietal tooth, and peristome of *H. inflecta* Say. Having a parietal tooth only, it is allied to *H. monodon* Rack; but independently of the form of the tooth being like that of *H. inflecta*, its closer relation to the latter is shown by the absence of the *fulcrum*, which is characteristic of the former. Being imperforate, and having the single tooth, this species is also allied to *H. germana* Gould, from Oregon, but it is less globose, and the epidermis and sculpturing are entirely different.

Helix Wheatleyi, nov. sp.

Plate IV. fig. 7.

T. imperforatà, depresse conoideo-globosâ, tenuiusculâ, rufescente-corneâ, conferte costulato-striatâ, sub lente minute granulatâ, pilis brevissimis ornatâ; spirâ breviter conoideâ; suturâ valde impressâ; anfr. 5½, convexiusculis, ultimo rotundato, ad aperturam breviter deflexo, constricto; basi convexo, circa columellam excavato; aperturâ obliquâ, lunari, pariete aperturali tuberculo dentiformi parvo munito; perist. acuto, roseo-labiato, æqualiter angulatim reflexo, columellari adnato.

Shell imperforate, depressed, conoid-globose, thin, reddish horn-colored, with numerous rib-like striæ, and microscopic granulations with very short hairs ; spire shortly conoid ; suture deeply impressed ; whorls 5½, rather convex, the last rounded, slightly depressed at the aperture, constricted ; base convex, excavated in the umbilical region ; aperture oblique, lunate, with a small parietal tooth-like tubercle ; peristome acute, rose-colored, equally angularly reflected, appressed at the columella. Diam. maj. 14, min. 12, Alt. 7, mill.

Habitat.—The mountains in Cherokee Co., N.Car., D. Christy !

Remarks.—This interesting species is in form and size most like a small variety of *H. Mitchelliana* Lea, or, the parietal tooth considered, an imperforate specimen of *H. bucculenta* Gould, but is especially distinct from both in its rufous color, granulated and hirsute surface, and excavated umbilical region.

This is the only known hirsute member, found east of the Rocky Mountains, of the sub-genus Patera Albers. *H. labiosa* Gould, which inhabits Oregon, is the only hirsute representative of that sub-genus on the western side of the mountains.

I am indebted to Mr. David Christy of Cincinnati for this and the preceding, and also specimens of other somewhat rare species found in the same region, viz. *H. barbigera* Redf. ; *H. Elliotti* Redf. ; *H. Clarkii* Lea, &c.

I dedicate this species to my esteemed friend Mr. C. M. Wheatley, author of the first general catalogue of the Shells of the United States, a zealous Naturalist, and generous contributor to the cabinets of others.

Helix lævigata Rafinesque.

Synonymy.

Helix *lævigata Fer.* Prod. 221,		1821.
—— *inornata Say.* Jl. Acad. Phil. II. 370, June,		1822.
—— " *Griffith* in sched.! fide Pfr.		

Helix *lævigata Fer.* Hist. t. 82, f. 6,   1822 !

—— *fuliginosa Binney* Bost. Jl. III. 417 (excl. desc. syn. et fig.) 1840.

—— *lævigata Chemn.* ed. II. Helix No. 522. t. 84, fig. 17–19, 1846 !

——   "   *Pfr.* Mon. Hel. I. No. 142,   1848.

—— *lucubrata Binney* Terr. Moll. II. 225, t. 32,   1851.

—— *lævigata Desh.* in Fer. Hist. I. p. 94.

—— *inornata Reeve,* No. 666,   1852.

—— *lævigata*   "   No. 672 ? ex parte,   1852.

—— *inornata Say,* W. G. Binney's Reprint, p. 24,   1856.

—— *lævigata W. G. Binney* Suppl. Terr. Moll. p. 108,   1859.

The following is Say's Description :—

H. inornata.—Shell subglobose, pale yellowish horn color, polished ;
whorls 5, rounded, wrinkled ; spire convex ; suture not deeply impressed ;
umbilicus small, profound ; aperture wide, at the junction of the labia
with the penultimate whorl shorter than the width of the mouth ;
labrum simple.

Inhabits Pennsylvania. Greatest width less than seven-tenths of an
inch.

This species has a strong resemblance to *H. ligera,* but in addition to
its superior magnitude, its aperture is proportionally wider, a character
which of course gives the whorls a greater breadth ; the whorls are also
fewer in number, and the distance between the terminations of the lips
is very perceptibly less than the width of the aperture, the reverse of
which obtains in the *ligera.*

In my Remarks, Annals of the Lyceum, Vol. VI., p. 352, I
expressed my belief that *H. inornata* Say is the same as *H.
lævigata* Raf., and not the *H. inornata* of Dr. Binney. My
friend Mr. W. G. Binney has since examined the subject in his
Supplement to the " Terrestrial Mollusks," and concludes that
his father's determination is correct.

It is not surprising that the question at this date is full of
difficulty, considering that a few years only after Say's death
Dr. Binney treated *fuliginosa* Griff., *lucubrata* Say, and *lævigata* Raf., as one species,—that Mr. Phillips, Curator of the

Museum of the Philadelphia Academy, labelled *lævigata* Raf. as *inornata* Say, but now states that his determinations were conjectural, while Dr. Griffith concurred at least in the repudiated label of *inornata* Say. Little confidence can be placed in the opinion given by Griffith as to the original specimen of *glaphyra* being one of *cellaria*, inasmuch as he sent examples of the latter to Dr. Ravenel under the name of *fuliginosa!*

Mr. Binney (Supp. p. 110) refers to the suggestion of an anonymous writer in Silliman's Journal (1837). In connexion with the foregoing, the following quotation of the writer's language is interesting, showing, as it does, the origin of the opinion :—"*H. glaphyra* and *inornata* Say, and *fuliginosa* Griffith, are only different ages of the same shell, if the specimens I have received from the Philadelphia conchologists be labelled correctly."

In Férussac's cabinet *inornata* Say is represented by *lævigata* Raf., and the latter by the same shell, and *fuliginosa* Griff. Deshayes remarks that he has doubts as to *lævigata*, having received it from America under the name of *inornata* Say. Pfeiffer refers to specimens of *lævigata* sent from this country as *inornata* Say, and to *inornata* By., and *fuliginosa* Griff. sent as *glaphyra* Say.

I find from original papers now in my possession, that Say, with his first letter to Férussac, sent a number of shells, and in the accompanying list of them, *H. glaphyra* is mentioned.

Férussac, in a letter dated July 15, 1820, acknowledged receipt of the shells, and of Say's publications, remarking, however, as to *H. glaphyra*, " Vous ne me l'avez pas envoyée, mais je soubconne comme vous, Monsieur, que c'est l'analogue de notre *H. nitens*, ou *cellaria* de Müller." In the same letter Férussac asks for examples of *H. glaphyra*, and gives a list of shells forwarded to Say, among which was *H. cellaria*.

Say in his reply (of which I have before me notes, without date, in his hand-writing) observed,—" *H. glaphyra*. I am sorry that I cannot send you a specimen yet, but next season I hope to have more leisure than I had last, and shall probably be able to procure it for you, as well as some species of Limax."

In January, 1821, Say's description of *H. ligera* was published,—he observed that it " approaches nearest to *H. glaphyra*."

In October, 1822, Say wrote, with European shells, to Mr. Stephen Elliott, and in the list of them I find " *H. cellaria* L."

It must be supposed that Say knew the shell called *fuliginosa*, but in 1832 he expressed ignorance of it.

In that year Mr. Robert Peter was in correspondence with Say, and sent him a list of shells collected near Pittsburg, Pa., enumerating among them *H. glaphyra*, and *H. fuliginosa*. Say's answer may be inferred from Peter's letter to him of 30th Dec., expressing surprise that Say did not know the name *fuliginosa*, which he, Peter, supposed had been published, and which he had from Dr. Green of Philadelphia. Peter, in the letter referred to, which, through the kindness of Mrs. Say, is now in my possession, endeavored to enlighten Say by explaining that *H. fuliginosa* " resembles *H. glaphyra* Vobis, but is a distinct shell, being about twice as large, having a larger umbilicus, and being of a dark horn or fuliginous color, without any of the thickening or whitish appearance beneath, which characterizes that shell ; in other respects it is very similar."

Peter, a Western naturalist, apparently instructed from Philadelphia, evidently referred *glaphyra* to *inornata* By.

All these circumstances seem to me very strongly to favor the belief not only that *glaphyra* and *cellaria* were known by Say to be distinct, but that his *glaphyra* is identical with *H. inornata* Binney, the *inornata* Say being another species.

Say could not have described *H. cellaria* in the language employed with respect to *glaphyra*, which, however, is perfectly applicable to the *Pennsylvanian* form of *inornata* By. Moreover, Say's description of *inornata* cannot be referred to Dr. Binney's shell.

In my cabinet are specimens of *H. lævigata* from N. Carolina, which in every particular—in form, size, color, and sculpture—agree with Say's diagnosis of *inornata*, and are justly comparable, especially as regards the base, with *H. ligera*.

Say mentions Pennsylvania as the habitat of his *inornata*,—it very probably occurs there, having been found in Maryland and Virginia, and also in Illinois.

Information afforded to me by Dr. Edmund Ravenel of Charleston, throws some light on all this mystery, if indeed it does not explain it.

Having through Dr. Ravenel cleared up some difficulties about *H. avara*, I inquired of him as to *H. inornata* Say, sending him a copy of my Notes on *H. glaphyra*, and specimens in illustration of my views, viz. *H. lævigata* under the name of *inornata* Say, and *H. inornata* By. under that of *H. glaphyra* Say.

On the 4th Feb., 1860, Dr. Ravenel wrote as follows:—

" The shell which you have now sent me as *H. inornata* Say is identical with my shells which I sent to Mr. Say with this name, and which he returned to me without comment. After receiving these shells from Mr. Say, having no doubt upon the matter, I distributed the shell to my correspondents, with this name, and Mr. Lea has recently written to me, that he has specimens now in his cabinet from me, with my original label, *H. inornatus.* Dr. Binney was with me, after my communication with Mr. Say, and must have seen the specimens in my cabinet, and I suppose that I sent him some.

" The shell which Mr. Binney has now sent to me as the 'true inornata,' is identical with the one you have sent as 'inornata Binney,' and which you believe to be *glaphyra.* I have not had this shell in my cabinet before.

" Griffith sent me two specimens many years ago labelled '*fuliginosa, from Pa.*' Some years after I received from England a dozen specimens of *cellaria;* on comparing these with Griffith's shells, I could see no difference. The two specimens from Griffith, and one of the British shells, I sent recently to Mr. W. G. Binney, and he returned them as *cellaria.*

"I am inclined to believe that Mr. Say's indisposition to *multiply species* induced him to unite the three shells,* with which we are now confused, under the one name *inornata*, and if it was not for the word *polished*, I would believe that my shell was the type from which his description was written. All of these shells are, I believe, found in Pennsylvania, certainly *inornata* By. and *fuliginosa*, and we can scarcely believe that they escaped the observation of so industrious a naturalist as Mr. Say. We have a similar instance of his uniting allied species in the *avara* group, in which he certainly embraced *H. Postelliana* and *espiloca*, and probably others which do not correspond with the description of the Florida *avara*."

Having heard it attributed to Say, that he never volunteered to correct errors, and even avoided indicating the shell (when directly applied to) intended by his description, I had further correspondence with Dr. Ravenel, who, under date 10th April, 1860, favored me with an explanatory letter, from which I extract the following :—

"In answer to your question whether Say ever corrected labels, I can tell you that I sent him the *H. Hopetonensis* without a name, merely writing 'Helix —— S. Car.,' and he returned some of the specimens with my label filled up 'H. tridentata var. ephabus Say.' I sent him specimens of a variety of the same, from the gardens in Charleston ; he then wrote in pencil on my label, 'H. tridentata var. ephabus,—the same as the shell which you sent me several years ago.' I sent him *H. Postelliana* with my label 'Helix —— S. Car.,' and he filled up the gap with 'avara Say.' With *H. espiloca* the same thing occurred. He corrected, and also gave me names of our marine shells sent to him ; and when I sent him new shells, he described them, and generally returned the specimens with his paper. I therefore infer and believe that if he had considered my label *H. inornata* incorrect, he would have corrected it ; and at the same time, if he had not considered the shell to be *inornata*, he would certainly have described it as new.

"I have before expressed the opinion to you that Mr. Say sometimes

---

* Dr. Ravenel overlooks *H. glaphyra Say*, but his explanatory suggestions are both interesting and valuable.

grouped allied species under one name, as with *H. auriculata* and *avara*, and this is only another instance. He was certainly acquainted with *inornata* By., our *inornata* Say, and *fuliginosa*, yet we have only *from him* the one name, *inornata.*

"I have no doubt that I derived the name *inornata* Say, which I used, from Mr. Stephen Elliott, who was in very frequent communication with Mr. Say."*

I may mention that I have letters, dated in 1822, from Mr. S. Elliott to Mr. Say, with copies, in his hand-writing, of the replies, which give very full notes on the shells sent by the former, but unfortunately not on the species now under consideration.

On the evidence thus brought together, I think myself not only justified but called upon to pronounce *II. lævigata* Raf. and *II. inornata* Say to be identical. The former name, without description, was published by Férussac in his Prodromus at about the same time as the latter by Say in the Journal of the Academy, but seeing that the shell is now better known as *II. lævigata*, and that doubts may still exist in the minds of some, it may be best to place Say's name in the synonymy of that species.

As the evidence with respect to *glaphyra* is somewhat less conclusive, I propose to let it stand in the synonymy of *II. inornata* By., retaining that name for the shell which Dr. Binney determined to be the *inornata* of Say.

Many of the species of this continent are extremely variable, and the description of any one form is not only unsatisfactory, but productive of much error. Say wrote under serious disadvantages as compared with authors of the present day, but his descriptions are remarkably accurate; and when I find a shell to which one of his specific names has been affixed not agree-

---

* Dr. Ravenel in another letter says, "I think that Say was cautious in his communications,]but that he would give his opinion of any species, when requested to do so. He was however very much more reserved in giving specimens away, —he certainly gave them to Mr. Elliott, but I have not a single specimen given to me by Mr. Say[from his Cabinet.'

ing with his description, I do not pronounce it faulty, but assume that sooner or later a form such as he must have had before him will come under my notice.

H. lævigata is a very variable species,—the following forms are in my cabinet:—

a. Diam. maj. 14, min. 12, Alt. 7 mill.   *Hab.* unknown.
b. "   " 17 " 14 " 8 "   " N. Carolina.
     pale yellowish horn colored, polished, irregularly striated,
     " wrinkled."
c. Diam. maj. 17, min. 14, Alt. 6 mill.   *Hab.* Maryland.
     in sculpturing much like var. *b.*
d. Diam. maj. 24, min. 20, Alt. 7 mill.   *Hab.* Georgia.
     regularly striated—last whorl with microscopic spiral lines
     on the upper surface.
e. Diam. maj. 26, min. 22, Alt. 9 mill.   *Hab.* Middle Georgia.
     very finely striated—microscopic elevated points in spiral
     lines on the upper and under surface of the last whorl—
     shell very thin; umbilicus larger than in other forms, and
     aperture more rounded; the entire shell of the same color,
     —in the other varieties the base is of lighter color than
     the upper surface. This is allied in form to *H. fuliginosa*
     Griff.
f. Diam. maj. 13, min. 20, Alt. 7 mill.   *Hab.* Georgia.
     striæ above like var. *d*, but they are continued over the
     periphery to the umbilical excavation.
g. Diam. maj. 23, min. 20, Alt. 9 mill.   *Hab.* St. Augustine, Florida.
     shell polished, sculpturing like var. *b*, the color of the upper
     surface as dark as *H. fuliginosa*,—beneath pale.

Helix inornata Binney.

SYNONYMY.

Helix *glaphyra Say?* Nich. Enc. IV. t. 1, f. 3,	1816.
inornata By. Bost. Jl. III. p. 419, t. 21, f. 3,	1840.
glaphyra Pfr. Mon. I. No. 120,	1848.
inornata By. Terr. Moll. II. p. 227, t. 34,	1851.

Helix *glaphyra* Rv. Conch. Icon. No. 667,   1852.
  inornata W. G. By. Suppl. p. 109,   1859.
  " *Pfr.* Mon. IV. No. 273,   1859.

In my remarks on *H. glaphyra* Say (Ann. Lyc. VI. 352), and in the preceding pages, I have fully stated my reasons for determining that *H. lævigata* Raf. and *H. inornata* Say are identical, and that *H. inornata* By. must be referred to *H. glaphyra* Say. To my mind the evidence is conclusive, but, as already explained, I leave the last named shell in the synonymy of *inornata* By.

I would repeat that, confining myself strictly to the *descriptions* of Say, I find that of his *inornata* applicable only to the shell known as *lævigata* Raf., and that of *glaphyra* only to the *inornata* By. Too much weight has been attached to the localities given by Say of his two shells. He attributes *inornata* to Pennsylvania, from whence we have now no authentic specimens, but the species occurs in Virginia and Maryland, and may reasonably be looked for on the borders at least of the adjoining state. *H. glaphyra* was found where certainly it was a stranger—no one knows how, or from whence it came. *H. cellaria*, to which it is referred, inhabits the New England States only, and the facts already stated indicate that Say knew *cellaria*, and in correspondence did not allude to it as his *glaphyra*.

H. inornata By. is a variable species. In many cabinets, both here and in Europe, it appears to be represented by specimens from Ohio, which, when mature, are generally by no means "very much depressed," and scarcely "pellucid, polished." I have individuals from N. Car. and also from Lycoming Co., Pa., which are planulate, pellucid, and with a very brilliant glassy polish. The Pennsylvanian form is small, and the color above is occasionally as dark as in *H. fuliginosa*. A young specimen with four whorls is much like Say's figure of *glaphyra*.*

---

* See Say's description of *H. glaphyra*, p. 42.

The following are measurements of specimens in my cabinet:
Diam. maj. 18, min. 15, alt. 7 mill.   Ohio.
   "   " ˙15   " 13 " 5 "   Maryland.
   "   " 14   " 12 " 5 "   Lycoming Co., Pa.
I have recently received from Dr. Ravenel, for examination,
a singular specimen, collected by himself on the mountains
near Ashville, N. Car., which I can only refer to this species.
It has 6 whorls, and measures,—
Diam. maj. 20, min. 18, Alt. 9 mill.

Helix friabilis W. G. Binney.

SYNONYMY.

Helix *friabilis* *W. G. Binney*, Proc. A. N. S. Phila. p. 187,   1857.
——   ——   "   Suppl. p. 106,   1859.
—— *lucubrata* *Pfr.* Mon. Hel. IV. No. 413, p. 68,   1859.

I concur with Mr. Binney in the establishment of this species,
but by no means with Dr. Pfeiffer in his view that it is the
II. lucubrata Say, with the description of which it does not
agree. Say mentions that *lucubrata* is closely allied to his
inornata, but *II. friabilis* is totally distinct both from *II. lævigata* Raf. and *II. inornata* By. W. G. Binney's shell is of uniform
color, and the umbilicus is not "much larger" than that of
either of the species referred to. The spire is not "much
depressed."

Binney describes the shell as having four whorls, but I have
seen no adult with less than five. Specimens from Illinois are
very thin, but those collected by Mrs. Say in Indiana, by Moore
in Texas, and received by Dr. Newcomb from De Witt Co. in
the latter state, are rather less so. I am indebted to Mr. Henry
Van Nostrand for a large and heavy example, having 5½
whorls, from Helena, Arkansas, the measurements of which are
as follows:—
Diam. maj. 31, min. 27, Alt. 16 mill.   Ap. 18 mill. longa,
15 lata.

Helix lucubrata Say.

This species was described by Say in the "New Harmony Disseminator of Useful Knowledge," II. 229 (July, 1829), and the description was republished by Mrs. Say in 1840, in "Descriptions of some New Terr. and Fluv. Shells of N. America." The subjoined copy is from the reprint of W. G. Binney.

"*H. lucubrata.* Shell subglobose, depressed, reddish brown, polished, subtranslucent; whorls over four, much wrinkled; spire much depressed, convex; suture moderate; beneath paler; umbilicus open, rather large; aperture nearly orbicular; labrum simple.

"Greatest width one inch. Inhabits Mexico. Closely allied to *H. inornata* Nob., but the umbilicus is much larger, and the aperture is more accurately rounded; the color is nearly the same, excepting that in the present it is of a deeper shade."

There is great difference of opinion as to this species, and indeed it has not been satisfactorily determined.

As has been shown, Dr. Binney confounded it with *H. lævigata*, by others it has been placed with that species in the synonymy of *H. fuliginosa*, and Pfeiffer has recently determined it to be the species described by W. G. Binney as *H. friabilis*.

Mr.. Binney (Suppl. p. 106) considers the Mexican *H. caduca* Pf. allied to, if not identical with it, and refers to "Mexican specimens of *lucubrata* preserved for many years in the Philadelphia Academy" as agreeing perfectly with that species.

I have critically examined the three specimens at the Academy; they are attached to a card, and labelled, by Mr. Phillips I believe, "Helix lucubrata Say, Mexico. N. H. Disseminator, vol. ii. p. 229." One of the specimens, that of which the base only is visible, is I think a pale var. of *H. fuliginosa*, but the other two differ from all the forms of the group, including *H. caduca Pf.*, which I have seen. The adult specimen (the other is young of the same) of which both the upper and lower side, and aperture can be fully seen, agrees *entirely* with Say's description of *H. lucubrata*, so much so as to favor the conclusion that it is an authentic example, if not indeed his type. It is appropriately compared with *H. lævigata Raf.* (*inornata Say*), but as Say remarks, the umbilicus is "much larger," nearly equal to that of *H. fuliginosa*, and the aperture "more accurately rounded," being somewhat wider, but much like that of Griffith's species. The shell is in color darker above than usual in *H. lævigata*, the darker shade extending over the periphery and terminating abruptly, where the paler color of the base prevails. The margin of the last whorl, at the suture, has indications of a line of a deeper reddish brown color than that of the rest of the upper surface of the shell.

The incremental striæ are well defined "wrinkles," but of irregular elevation, and not equidistant. The shell has five whorls, less rapidly increasing than in *H. lævigata*, and the following are its dimensions:—

Diam. maj. 26, min. 23, Alt. 11½ mill. Ap. 12 mill. long. 12 lat.

This Academy specimen differs from examples of *H. caduca Pf.* received from Mr. Cuming and M. Sallé in the following particulars; it is more strongly "wrinkled," of darker color above, and the aperture is more orbicular—the last whorl is more ventricose.

A specimen of *H. caduca* in my cabinet, with 5¼ whorls, measures, Diam. maj. 26, min. 21½, Alt. 10 mill. Ap. 10 mill. long. 13 lat. The color is scarcely paler at the base than above, the umbilicus is the same as in the Academy shell, and the whorls increase in the same proportion. Several young shells have the same but more plainly discernible dark sutural line.

Considering the Philadelphia specimen to be the *H. lucubrata Say*, I cannot pronounce it to be identical with *H. caduca*, but intermediate between it and *H. lævigata*—more closely allied to the former, and possibly a variety of it, certainly distinct from the latter and from *H. fuliginosa*, and *H. friabilis*.

Helix septemvolva Say.

This species was described by Say in Nicholson's Enc. in 1816,* and the description was republished in the Journal of the Philadelphia Academy in May 1818 ; it is as follows :—

" P. SEPTEMVOLVA.—Shell much depressed, discoidal; spire not prominent; whorls seven, perfectly lateral, compressed, depressed, and marked with conspicuous lines and grooves above, a projecting carina on the upper edge of the body whorl, beneath which the lines and grooves are obsolete; aperture subreniform, not contracted ; lips equal elevated, outer one reflected, regularly rounded so as to describe two-thirds of a circle; pillar lip projecting inwards, into an angle or tooth, which is concave beneath; beneath the four exterior volutions equally prominent, transverse diameters equal to those of the upper surface; umbilicus central, moderate, attenuated to the apex so as to exhibit the remaining volutions.

Breadth, female, two-fifths—male, three-tenths of an inch. Inhabits Georgia and East Florida. Cabinet of the Academy. A very common shell in many parts of Georgia, particularly the sea islands, also in East Florida. We found them numerous under the ruins of old Fort Picolata on the St. John River, and on the Oyster-shell Hammocks, near the sea, and in other situations under decaying palmetto logs, roots, &c."

This is a very variable shell, and the species of the group to which it belongs, inhabiting the Southern States and adjacent Islands and Keys, as well as the Bahama and Bermuda Islands, have not been accurately defined and determined.

Say, it may be inferred, considered all the individuals which came under his notice from the United States as belonging to *septemvolva.* He sent specimens to Férussac, and was informed, by letter in reply dated 15th July, 1820, that the species had been figured and described in 1816, by Megerle de Muhlfeldt in the Berlin Magazine, under the name of *H. cereolus.*

---

* Mr. Binney mentions in the Preface to the reprint of Say's writings on the Conchology of the United States, that he had not been able to find the first edition of this work, but gives its date 1816, on the authority of Férussac, Mag. de Zool. 1835.

The description by Muhlfeldt (Berlin Mag. VIII. p. 41, pl. ii.
fig. 18, 1816) is short, and the figure indifferent,—I subjoin
copy of the former:—

"T. orbiculari, umbilicata, utrinque planata, alba, oblique subcostata,
marginata, unidentata."

The dimensions given are Diam. 4½ lines, Alt. about 1 line.
In some remarks (in German) Muhlfeldt mentions that the shell
has eight whorls, and that it was most probably from the West
Indies, specimens having been found with a lot of shells from
thence.

Deshayes (in Fer. Hist. I. p. 1839?) remarks in connexion
with *H. septemvolva :*

"Il est bien à présumer que l'*H. cercolus* de Megerle est la même
que celle-ci; cependant sa description trop courte et sa figure médiocre-
ment exécutée, nous laissent quelques doutes sur son identité avec celle
que nous venons de décrire."

Deshayes (in Fer. Hist. I. p. 6, pl. 72, fig. 13) described *H.
microdonta* as follows :

T. discoidea, planulata, albo-grisea, flammulis obliquis fuscis sub-
rubescentibusve ornata ; superne spira depressissima, subtus profunde
lateque in ambitu umbilicata, tenuissime et regulariter striata ; apertura
obliqua, marginata, ovato-semilunari ; labio dente obliquo minimo præ-
dito.

Hab.—L'Amerique méridionale ? l'isle de Cuba ? communiquée à M.
de Férussac par M. d'Orbigny.

Nous n'avons sous les yeux que le seul individu de cette espèce que
possédoit la coll. de M. de Férussac ; nous le regardons comme appar-
tenant à une espèce bien distincte, intermédiaire par ses caractères entre
l'*H. septemvolva* et le *lingulata* (*paludosa Pf.*) se rapprochant cependant plus de cette dernière que de l'autre. Elle est orbiculaire, depri-
mée, à spire à peine saillante au-dessus du dernier tour ; mais elle n'est
pas concave en dessus ; en dessous la coquille est percée d'un ombilic
profond et s'élargissant subitement à son entrée, parce que le dernier tour

se déroule par une spire plus large que ceux qui le précèdent. Les tours de spire au nombre de sept sont convexes, couverts de stries fines, regulieres, rapprochées, plus profondes sur le côté supérieur que dans la partie ombilicale : elles s'attenuent insensiblement en passant du dessus à la circonférence et de la circonférence au-dessous. L'ouverture est très oblique, le bord droit, épaissi en dedans, est renversé en dehors ; il se continue par ses extremités en un bord gauche, sur le milieu duquel se relève une petite dent oblique et courbée que l'on voit tout entière en dehors lorsque l'on regarde l'ouverture de profil. Cette coquille est d'un blanc grisâtre, et elle est ornée de flammules longitudinales, etroites, irrégulièrement distribuées et d'un brun pâle et rougeâtre.

"Elle a 10 mill. de diamètre et 4 de hauteur."*

Pfeiffer (Mem. i. p. 409, 1848) assigns *H. microdonta* to the Bermudas and Texas, " teste coll. Menkeana."

Muhlfeldt and Deshayes did not know the localities from which their specimens came—the figure and description of the former author are unsatisfactory, and the latter described from a single individual, and gives a figure which is by no means conclusive. Under such circumstances, considering that the species of the group to which *H. cereolus* and *H. microdonta* belong are very variable, it is not surprising that difficulty should be now experienced in determining them.

When in Bermuda, in 1852, I collected a large number of specimens of a finely striated shell, pretty closely agreeing with the description of *H. microdonta Desh.;* but Mr. Shuttleworth, in 1855, was disposed to think it distinct, and proposed to call it *H. delitescens,* under which name it has been extensively distributed, but nothing published about it.

In 1853, Mr. S. sent me specimens labelled " *H. microdonta* Desh., Key West, Florida," which differ very much from the Bermuda shell, having sharp and more distant striæ, and an internal lamella. I also received from the same source examples of *H. volvoxis* Parr., from Hopeton, Ga. Both these

---

* See facsimile of the figure to which Deshayes refers, in W. G. Binney's Supp. to the Terr. Moll., pl. 78, fig. 23.

species were at that time apparently unknown to American conchologists. Dr. Binney makes no mention of them in the Terr. Moll. ; and Dr. Gould even omits them in vol. iii. (1857), although he inserts descriptions of additional species, " so as to embody all the species at present known." Mr. W. G. Binney admits them in the Supplement (1859) to his father's work.

In 1859, Mr. Wm. Cooper collected at Nassau, New Providence, numerous specimens of a species apparently identical, though varying somewhat from that which inhabits Bermuda.*

Neither Mr. Binney nor I have received, or even seen specimens from Texas of any of the species belonging to this group.

Before examining the strictly North American species in detail, I may explain that I consider *H. cereolus* Mühl. and *H. septemvolva* Say to be distinct,—that the Bermuda shell is the *H. microdonta* Desh, and that the species from Florida, now known here as *microdonta*, has not been described. In the following pages I describe it under the name of *H. Carpenteriana*. As to *H. volvoxis* Parr. I think that it is no more than var. of *H. septemvolva*.

H. septemvolva, as *described* by Say, cannot be misunderstood,—it occurs only, I believe, in East Florida, and especially at and in the vicinity of St. Augustine,—for many fine specimens collected there, I am indebted to Mr. O. M. Dorman. It is variable in size, but distinguished by its sharp carina and open umbilicus. In a specimen with 8½ whorls (diam. maj. 14 mill.), the width of the actual umbilical opening is 2 mill. The penultimate beneath is generally half covered by the last whorl. The very small var., called the *male* by Say, is comparatively rare.

The four examples preserved at Philadelphia, said to be authentic, are of the form described.

---

* *H. paludosa* Pf. (*lingulata* Fer.), an inhabitant of Cuba and Jamaica (rare in the latter island), belongs to this group, but is readily distinguished by its rugose upper surface, and small parietal tooth which is unconnected with the margins of the peristome.

The following are measurements of large and small specimens in my cabinet:—

Diam. maj. 14, min. 12½ mill., Alt. 3 mill. anf. 8½.
 "   "   7½ "   6½ "   " 2½ "   " 7.

Associated with *septemvolva*, Mr. Dorman found not only the shell described by Pfeiffer as *H. volvoxis*, but an intermediate form, in which the flat upper surface and carina of the former, are combined with the more tumid character, and breadth of the last whorl beneath of the latter. In many specimens the uniform opaque light color of the base of each whorl is a striking feature. Mr. Dorman informs me that in some places in St. Augustine the three forms are found together, but that *septemvolva* and *volvoxis* generally inhabit different localities.

Helix volvoxis Parreyss.

Pfeiffer's description of this species is as follows:—

T. umbilicata, orbiculato-convexa, tenuis, rufo-cornea, pellucida, regulariter costulato-striata; spira brevissima, convexa; anfr. 7 convexi, regulariter accrescentes, ultimus reliquis superne vix latior, angulatus, infra angulum inflatus, striatus, nitidus; umbilicus latus, regularis, anfractu ultimo latissimo, reliquis regulariter decrescentibus; apertura majuscula, reniformis; perist. intus callosum, reflexum, marginibus callo brevi, triangulari, dentiformi junctis. Diam. maj. 9, min. 8; Alt. 4, mill. Habitat in America boreali: Georgia, Florida.

Obs. Hanc speciem, a præcedente (H. cereolus Mühl.) toto cœlo diversam, sæpius ex America nomine H. septemvolvæ Say accepimus.

This shell is very generally labelled in cabinets *H. septemvolva*, but I entertain great doubts, looking at my extensive suite of specimens, as to its specific difference.

The form described by Pfeiffer is common in St. Simon's Island, Ga., whence I have examples collected by Mr. Postell.

It varies in size,—the following are the measurements of a small specimen, having 6½ whorls:—

Diam. maj. 7½, min. 6½; Alt. 3 mill.

Helix cereolus Mühlfeldt.

I have already quoted the original description of this species at page 133, and refer to the copy of the author's unsatisfactory figure, published by W. G. Binney in his Suppl. pl. 77, fig. 23. The *whitish* shell, *H. cereolus Mühl.* var. *luminifera* of W. G. Binney's catalogue in the Philadelphia Proceedings, which we have in our cabinets, found by Lieut. Wurdeman at Indian River, E. Florida, and also from Indian Key, belongs in my opinion to this species. The annexed figures,* double the natural size, of the base of *septemvolva* (fig. 1.) and *cereolus* (fig. 2.) show the striking differences in the characters of the umbilicus, and of the aperture, and also that Mühlfeldt's figure, especially of the umbilicus, agrees rather with the latter than the former.

FIG. 1.   FIG. 2.

H. septemvolva Say.   *H. cereolus Mühl.*

The umbilical opening, in specimens of about equal size, is only half the width of that in *septemvolva ;* the last whorl is wider, especially towards its termination at the aperture, more inflated, and rather less acutely carinated. The aperture is more orbicular, more contracted, and the outer lip more expanded

---

* The woodcuts were executed by Waters & Son, 90 Fulton Street, New York, admirable figures of the shells having been previously photographed, in their establishment, on the block. I gladly avail myself of this opportunity of calling the attention of naturalists to this valuable method of securing accurate figures.

and acutely reflected, and at its junction below with the pillar lip more closely appressed to the last whorl.

This shell has generally a more or less developed internal lamina, commencing on the parietal side of the inner fourth of the last, and running round rather obliquely within from two-thirds to three-fourths of the penultimate whorl,—revolving in fact nearly once round the shell.

In some specimens the penultimate whorl below is partially covered by the last, as in *septemvolva.*

This species, which I consider distinct from *H. septemvolva* Say, has from 7 to 8 whorls, and measures as follows :—

Diam. maj. 14, min. 12½, Alt. 3½ mill. (large specimen.)

"   "   9, "   8 " 2½ " (small do.)

Dr. Gould (Terr. Moll. Vol. III. p. 31) refers to the vertical series on Plate XXXVIII as reprenting the typical form of *H. septemvolva* Say, but the lower figure, showing the base, is certainly not of the shell *described* by Say, rather of that which I call *H. cereolus.*

Helix Carpenteriana, nov. sp.

SYNONYMY.

Helix *microdonta* *Pfr.* Mon. 1. p. 499 ex-parte ?   1848.
—— ———— *W. G. Binney,* Notes on Amer. Land Shells,
                                Phila. Proc.   1858.
—— ————   "   Suppl. Terr. Moll. p. 91,   1859.

T. umbilicatâ, orbiculatâ, corneâ vel pallide rufescente, superne planâ, oblique et argute costulatâ, subtus convexâ, leviter striatâ, nitidâ, maculis opacis, indistinctis, sæpe ornatâ; suturâ valde impressâ; anfr. 5½–6½, ultimo ad peripheriam superne subangulato, ad aperturam breviter sed subito deflexo, gibbosulo, scrobiculato-constricto, pone aperturam tumido, costulato, basi dilatato, laminâ internâ albâ in pariete columellari, pone aperturæ insertionem sitâ; aperturâ perobliquâ, lunari; perist. intus calloso, incrassato, reflexiusculo, marginibus lamellâ dentiformi triangulari junctis.

Shell umbilicate, orbicular, horn-colored or pale rufous, above flat, obliquely and acutely ribbed, beneath convex, slightly striated, shining, often ornamented with indistinct white spots; suture deeply impressed; whorls 5½–6½, the last subangular at the periphery, shortly but suddenly deflected at the aperture, gibbous, scrobiculate, constricted, tumid behind the aperture, and ribbed, base dilated, with a white internal lamina on the columellar wall near the point of attachment of the aperture; aperture very oblique, lunate; perist. callous within, thickened, little reflected, the margins joined by a triangular dentiform lamella.

Diam. maj. 10, min. 9, Alt. 4 mill. anfr. 6½.
"   "   7, " 6, " 3 "   " 5½.

Habitat.—Key Biscayne, Florida, Wurdeman! Key West, Shuttleworth. South Florida, Dr. Cooper! Sea Islands, Florida, Bartlett. Lake Harney, Fla., E. Norton!

Remarks.—This species has been hitherto named *H. micro-donta* Desh. in American Cabinets, and I have indeed so distributed it, but I believe erroneously. It is readily distinguished from all the other species of the group by its strong acute rib-like striæ, and the peculiarity of the outer whorl. About the last third of it, behind the aperture, is ribbed and tumid,—the whorl is then rather abruptly contracted, becoming narrower above, and flattened and slightly striated beneath, but again, as it passes towards and beneath the aperture, dilated, and convex. This change of form gives to the last whorl a distorted appearance. The internal lamina is on the columellar wall of the contracted and flattened portion of the last whorl, and runs obliquely, in the direction of the aperture, attaining a length in a large specimen of about 6 mill. The character of the aperture is most like that of *H. cereolus*, but in that species the last whorl has none of the peculiarities above described. The internal lamina is found in a majority of specimens, but not in all; it can generally be seen through the outer wall of the shell.

In my Cabinet are specimens, received from Mr. W. G. Binney, belonging to this species, having all the peculiarities of the last whorl, but being rather delicately striated,—they are extremely small, and were, I believe, from Dr. Binney's Cabinet; the habitat unknown. The measurements are,

Diam. maj. 5½, min. 5, Alt. 2 mill. anfr. 5.

The variety from Lake Harney is dark horn-colored, thin, translucent, acutely ribbed, but with little of the peculiarities of the last whorl prevailing in the Key Biscayne specimens, and in the small variety already noticed,—the whorl, scarcely flattened and contracted as in those, is nearly of uniform size beneath.

Several years ago I received from the late Mr. Clark of Cincinnati, about a dozen shells of the species now under consideration, labelled by Mr. Bartlett "H. septemvolva Say, Matanzas, Cuba," but agreeing with specimens sent to me by Mr. Shuttleworth as *H. microdonta* from Key West. I communicated them under the latter name to M. Poey, who seeing that live examples have not been found in Cuba, doubtfully refers the species to the fauna of that island. (Vide Mem. V. II. p. 49 and 90.)

This species I dedicate to my friend Mr. P. P. Carpenter, author of the "Report on the Present State of our Knowledge with regard to the Mollusca of the West Coast of North America," &c., &c., whose labors in the United States have added much to the value of many of our public and private cabinets.

NOTE.—H. MICRODONTA DESH.—With respect to this species, looking at his description, I cannot doubt but that the author refers to the Bermuda shell, now somewhat extensively known in cabinets as *H. delitescens* Shutt. I should mention that Mr. Shuttleworth, in his latest correspondence with me on the subject, expressed some doubt as to treating the Florida shell as the species described by Deshayes. Those doubts may account for the non-publication of *H. delitescens.*

The shells found in abundance by Mr. W. Cooper, at Nassau, agree rather with those from Bermuda than any other. But in one with very fine striæ (anfr. 6½), and in another (anfr. 7), with the striæ rather coarse, I have detected the internal lamina. In both, the outer whorl is without the characteristic features of *H. Carpenteriana*. Among a considerable number of specimens I found the lamina only in the two referred to. I have never seen it in the Bermuda shell, of which I have examined very many individuals.

The Bermuda shell was known to Say. He wrote a description, which was, however, never published. The following is a copy from the original MS. in the possession of Mr. Binney :

" H. CHEILODON.—Discoidal, labrum reflected—a tooth on the labium. Inhabits Bermuda.

" Shell discoidal, the spire very slightly convex, whorls nearly 6, with elevated striæ across, forming somewhat regular intervening grooves,—body whorl angular above its middle, beneath which it is convex, and only wrinkled, the grooves terminating at the angle or carina,—umbilicus dilated, exhibiting the volutions to the apex : aperture rather longer than wide,—labrum contracting the aperture a little, reflected, excepting towards its superior termination, and declining a little at its junction with the preceding volution : labium with a short, oblique tooth. Breadth, ⅔ inch. The late Mr. Stephen Elliott presented to me this shell, which he obtained from Bermuda. It is more completely fastigiate than even *H. septemvolva* Nob., and there is no obvious calcareous deposit on the labium, as in that species."

It may be remarked that Say's description agrees almost entirely with that of Deshayes of *microdonta*,—in specimens from Bermuda, not completely full grown, but with reflected lip, the labial tooth is of the character mentioned by Say.

HELIX FASTIGANS L. W. Say.—In my Remarks (Ann. Lyc. Vol. VI. p. 283) on *H. fatigiata* Say, I noticed that the name was originally written by Say correctly, viz. *fastigiata*, and that Pfeiffer had remarked to the effect that the former word is unmeaning. Mrs. Say, anxious that this long-standing typographical error should be removed, expresses her wish that the specific name of the species should be altered to *fastigans*, that of *fastigiata* having been applied by Hutton to another.

Helix porcina Say.—I commented on this species in Ann. Lyc. Vol. VI. p. 344, suggesting that Say's description applies rather to a young *H. inflecta*, than *H. hirsuta*, but anticipating that " further researches will prove this to be a distinct species." I now learn that *H. hispida* L. inhabits some parts of Nova Scotia, and also Canada East ; and Dr. Gould suggests —as indeed seems highly probable—that *H. porcina* is identical with it.

REMARKS

ON

CERTAIN SPECIES

OF

NORTH AMERICAN HELICIDÆ,

WITH

DESCRIPTIONS OF NEW SPECIES.

BY

THOMAS BLAND, F.G.S., LONDON,

MEMBER OF THE LYCEUM OF NATURAL HISTORY, NEW YORK; CORRESPONDING MEMBER OF THE
ACADEMY OF NATURAL SCIENCES, PHILADELPHIA, &C.

REPRINTED FROM THE ANNALS OF THE LYCEUM OF NATURAL HISTORY,
NEW YORK. VOL. VII.

PART III.   ·

NEW YORK:

BAILLIÈRE BROTHERS, 440 BROADWAY.

LONDON:—H. BAILLIÈRE, 219 REGENT STREET.

PARIS:—J. B. BAILLIÈRE ET FILS, RUE HAUTEFEUILLE.

MADRID:—C. BAILLY-BAILLIÈRE, CALLE DEL PRINCIPE.

1862.

CONTENTS.

DESCRIPTIONS OF NEW SPECIES.

REMARKS ON THE FOLLOWING SPECIES, VIZ. :

Remarks on Certain Species of North American HELICIDÆ.

BY THOMAS BLAND.

Read December 16th, 1861.

Reprinted from the Annals of the Lyceum of Natural History, New York, Vol. VII., December, 1861.

Helix Downieana nov. sp.

Plate IV. fig. 23–24.

T. subobtecte umbilicatâ, subglobosâ, tenui, subpellucidâ, obsolete costulato-striatâ, lineis spiralibus impressis sublente confertim decussatâ, virenti-corneâ; spirâ brevi, obtusâ; anfr. 5, convexis, ultimo tumido, antice gibbosulo, vix descendente, constricto; aperturâ obliquâ, lunato-ovali; perist. albo, labiato, reflexo, margine dextro expanso, columellari angulatim dilatato umbilicum fere tegente.

Shell umbilicate, umbilicus nearly covered, subglobose, thin, subpellucid, with obsolete rib-like striæ, decussated with crowded microscopic spiral lines, greenish horn-colored; spire short, obtuse; whorls five, convex, the last tumid, anteriorly somewhat gibbous, scarcely descending, constricted; aperture oblique, lunate-oval; perist. white, labiate, reflected, right margin expanded, columellar margin angularly dilated, nearly covering the umbilicus.

Diam. maj. 10½, min 9½, Alt. 6 mill.

Station.—Among leaves, at the roots of grass and shrubs in rocky places.

Habitat.—University Place, Franklin Co., Tenn. Downie!

Remarks.—In the autumn of 1860 I received three specimens, through Bishop Elliott, from Major Downie of Brunswick, Ga., to whom I dedicate the species. In form and aspect it is most like *H. Christyi* Nob., but has no parietal tooth; it is allied also to *H. clausa* Say, and *H. Mitchelliana* Lea.

Helix alternata Say.

The geographical distribution of the varieties of *H. alternata* is interesting. The species attains its largest size in Ohio and Michigan—from the former I have it with 6 whorls, Diam. maj. 24, min. 22, Alt. 10 mill. In both of those States individuals are found of nearly uniform color, from pale straw to dark reddish brown. In Canada, on Goat Island, Niagara, and on Cunningham Island, Lake Erie, the shell is frequently much elevated, even globose, thickened, and almost covered with dark-colored flammules.

A beautiful variety was discovered a few years ago by Mr. Ferguson on the Helderberg Mountains, New York; subsequently near Greenwood Cemetery, Long Island; and also in the woods adjoining the New York Bay Cemetery, near Jersey City. It is small, comparatively smooth, especially at the base, has a shining somewhat translucent epidermis, which on dead shells becomes opaque. The suture is well impressed and the outer whorl is not, as usual in the species, obsoletely carinated. The deep red flammules are disposed with much regularity on a pale horn-colored ground. An average sized specimen, with 5 whorls, is Diam. maj. 15½, min. 14, Alt. 6½ mill. The animal does not exude the saffron-colored mucous secretion usually observed in the typical form. I designate this shell as *H. alternata* Say var. *H. Fergusoni.*

In Tennessee, North and South Carolina, and Georgia, the moderately elevated and numerous striæ of *H. alternata* are replaced by sharply defined distant ribs. In a specimen from North Carolina, for which I am indebted to Mr. David Christy, these ribs have a remarkable development, being nearly 1 mill. apart on the last whorl; the shell is depressed, but obsoletely carinated only. Bishop Elliott found a few specimens on the eastern slope of the Cumberland Mountains, strongly ribbed, depressed, and the last whorl subcarinate, the carina in a measure obsolete behind the aperture, but modifying its form.

The var. found fossil at Jackson, Miss., is well marked; being ribbed above, the ribs passing over the periphery, with, at the base, an additional less prominent rib between each. I have living examples of the same form from Tennessee, Arkansas, and Louisiana.

Helix mordax Shuttleworth.

This was described by Shuttleworth in the following terms : (*Bern. Mitth.*, 1852, *Diag. n. Moll.*, No. 2.)

T. late et perspective umbilicata, depressa, sublenticularis, carinata, tenuis, luteo-cornea, strigis rufis interruptis fasciatim ornata, costis validis flexuosis remotis utrinque eximie asperata ; anfr. 5½, plani ; apertura perobliqua angulatim lunari-ovalis ; perist. simplex, acutum.

Diam. maj. 18, min. 16, Alt. 6 mill.

Hab.—In mont. Carolinæ sept. specimina ultra 12 legit Rugel.

Obs.—H. alternatæ valde affinis, sed costis validioribus, ad 1 mill. inter se remotis, distincta. H. Cumberlandiana Lea (forsan mere forma monstruosa), quâcum carina congruit, differt (ex icone) testa tantum tenuiter striata nec costata.

Shuttleworth observes that *H. mordax* being costate is distinct from *H. alternata*, and also from *H. Cumberlandiana*, described by Lea as *tenuiter striata ;* the fact is, that both his own and Lea's species are costate, although the costæ in the latter are not so sharp and regular, indeed on the last whorl near the aperture are partially obsolete. Shuttleworth states that his shell agrees, as regards the carina, with *H. Cumberlandiana.* I have not seen an authentic specimen of *H. mordax*, but looking at the description consider that it bears the same relation to *H. Cumberlandiana*, as *H. Carolinensis* to *H. obstricta*, and although with costæ like the southern forms of *H. alternata* already noticed, being carinated to the extent described, it is a variety of *H. Cumberlandiana.*

Helix Cumberlandiana Lea.

I subjoin a copy of Lea's description, (*Trans. Amer. Phil. Soc.*, VIII. *p.* 229, *pl.* 6, *fig.* 61, 1840.)

CARACOLLA CUMBERLANDIANA.

T. lenticulata, carinata, striata, albida, fusco-notata, latè umbilicata, ad carinam superne et inferne impressa; anfr. quinis; apertura angulata, intus sulcata; labro acuto.

Shell lenticular, carinate, striate, whitish, brown-spotted, widely umbilicate, impressed above and below the carina; whorls 5; aperture angular, within furrowed, lip acute.

Hab.—Cumberland Mts. near Jasper, Tennessee. Dr. Currey.

Diam. .54, length .14 inch.

Remarks.—Among many species of land shells which I owe to Dr. Currey's kindness, were two individuals of this Caracolla which does not appear to have been before noticed. It has some resemblance to *H. alternata* Say, but may at once be distinguished by its depressed, flat, lenticular form and carina. It is a very interesting species, and has a remarkable furrow above and below the carina; all the whorls are visible in the umbilicus, and are striate all over.

This beautiful species was extremely rare, even in American cabinets, until Bishop Elliott, after diligent search during several summers, discovered it in August, 1860, inhabiting a single spur of the Cumberland Mountains, near University Place, Franklin County, Tenn. In one of his letters to me he mentions having found it on the ground, under stones and wood, in company with *H. spinosa* Lea, and also after rain creeping upon precipitous faces of rock, with a few *H. alternata* (the common Southern form), and *Helicina orbiculata* Say. My largest specimen measures, Diam. maj. 17, min. 15, Alt. 5½ mill.

Helix tridentata Say.

This well known species varies much in size; for a very unusually large specimen, said to be from Tennessee, I am indebted to Mr. Henry Van Nostrand ; it measures,

Diam. maj. 23, min. 19, Alt. 9 mill. (6 whorls).

The comparatively smooth Ohio form is,

Diam. maj. 19, min. 16, Alt. 7 mill. (5½ whorls).

A small variety from Goat Island, N. Y., is,

Diam. maj. 13, min. 10½, Alt. 5½ mill. (5 whorls).

A variety found by Mr. H. Van Nostrand, at Delaware Water Gap, Pa., has very rigid somewhat distant ribs.

The position of the upper lip-tooth in this species is not absolutely constant, its distance from the lower one is variable.

Helix triodontoides nov. sp.

Plate IV. fig. 11–12.

T. perforatâ, globoso-depressâ, tenui, subpellucidâ, pallide corneâ, superne subobsolete costulato-striatâ, basi convexâ, lævigatâ ; spirâ brevi ; anfr. 5 convexiusculis, ultimo prope aperturam plicato, antice deflexo ; aperturâ rotundato-lunari, obliquâ, coarctatâ ; perist. reflexo, calloso, marginibus dente linguiformi, acuto, triangulari junctis, dextro dente in margine calli posito, basali dente obliquo munito, ambobus dentibus parvis, inter se remotis.

Shell perforate, globose-depressed, thin, subpellucid, pale horn-colored, with partially obsolete rib-like striæ above ; base convex, smooth ; spire short ; whorls 5, somewhat convex, the last plicately ribbed near the aperture, deflexed anteriorly ; aperture roundly lunate, oblique, contracted ; perist. reflected, callous, the margins joined by a sharp linguiform triangular tooth, the right with a tooth on the margin of the callus, basal with an oblique tooth, both teeth small and far apart.

Diam. maj. 9½, min. 8, Alt. 5 mill.

Habitat.—De Witt Co., Texas, Dr. Newcomb !; Corpus Christi, Texas.

Remarks.—It has been generally assumed that the *H. trio-*

donta Jan is identical with *H. Texasiana* Moricand. Férussac (Bul. Zool., 1853) states that it is so. Dr. Binney, looking at specimens bearing Jan's name in the Paris Museum, made the following note : " *H. triodonta* Jan is the shell which we have from Texas like *H. tridentata*, with very small teeth ; it seems to run into *H. Texasiana* Mor." Dr. Binney referred to the shell which I have above described; if Jan's shell is the same, it should bear the name given by him. W. G. Binney sent specimens to Pfeiffer, whose opinion is quoted (Terr. Moll. iv. 79, pl. 78, fig. 18), that it is var. of *H. Texasiana*, but Mr. Binney now concurs with me in considering it distinct.

H. triodontoides is a more delicate shell than *H. Texasiana*, and does not attain the same size. It is not as distinctly ribbèd, is somewhat more elevated, and the aperture is more round. The last whorl is less devious at its termination beneath, the lip teeth are smaller and wide apart. In *H. Texasiana* they are close together, and the space between them has much resemblance to the notch in *H. hirsuta*. In that respect, as well as in the form of the aperture, Moricand's shell is more closely allied to *H. Mooreana* W. G. By.

H. Texasiana varies much in size, which is not the case with my species. The following are measurements of specimens of the former in my cabinet :

Diam maj. 11½, min. 9, Alt. 5 mill.
"   "   8   "   7   "   4   "

Helix inflecta Say.

Say gives $\frac{9}{20}$ths of an inch as the greatest transverse diameter of this species ; the size and other characters are, however, variable. For an extraordinarily large specimen, found at University Place, Tenn., I am indebted to Bishop Elliott; having 5½ whorls, it measures, Diam. maj. 16, min. 14, Alt. 7 mill.

A small var., Diam maj. 9, min. 8, Alt. 4½ mill., inhabits Taylor Co., Ga. (Dr. Neisler), in which the superior tooth on the peristome is situated lower than in the typical form ; and in consequence the space between it and the inferior tooth is reduced.

From Darien, Ga. (Dr. Wilson !), and St. Simon's Island, Ga. (J. Postell !), I have a variety in which the epidermis has very little of the usual hirsute character; the aperture is more rounded, and the two lip teeth are small, in fact mere denticles. The parietal tooth is less oblique and more central, not being continued to the lower margin of the little reflected lip.

Helix Rugeli Shuttleworth.

The following is a copy of Shuttleworth's description of this species (*Diag. n. Moll., No.* 2, *p.* 18).

T. obtecte perforata, orbiculato-convexa, granulato-striata, parce setosa, corneo-cerea ; spira brevis, obtusa ; anfr. 5½, convexiusculi, ultimus antice subito deflexus, ad aperturam valde constrictus ; apertura depressa, dente valido linguiformi flexuoso in pariete aperturali intrante coarctata ; perist. reflexum, intus callosum, margine dextro dente magno obtuso profunde immerso extus subscrobiculato, basali dente minore transverso submarginali instructo.

Diam. maj. 13, min. 11½, Alt. 6¼ mill.

Hab.—In Tennessee (Rugel).

Obs.—Specimina plurima vidi. Variat magnitudine, sed semper major quam H. inflecta Say, cui maxime affinis ; differt insuper dente parietali magis evoluto et angulatim flexuoso, et dente supero marginis dextri peristomatis crasso et valde immerso.

As regards the form and position of the upper tooth on the lip, this species has the same connexion with *H. inflecta*, as *H. fallax* with *H. tridentata*.

Shuttleworth's measurements show that his species is not always larger than *H. inflecta*. The following are the dimensions of the largest and smallest specimens in my cabinet.

Diam. maj. 13½, min. 11½, Alt. 6 mill.   Cherokee Co. N. Car.
                                                    Christy !

       "   " 9   " 7 " 4½ "   '

Helix hirsuta Say.

This species varies in size ; in my cabinet are specimens which measure as follows :
Diam. maj. 11½, min. 10, Alt. 6½ mill.
"　　"　6　"　5　"　4　"
The last whorl in front of the aperture, especially in the larger forms, is more or less angulated, but I have never seen a specimen carinated. The position of the parietal tooth is often rather oblique, but usually nearly parallel with the lower lip, and is more or less distant from it. The nature of the epidermis varies ; in some forms the hairs are very numerous, in others comparatively few. Spiral impressed lines sometimes occur beneath the epidermis, at the base of the shell.

Helix stenotrema Férussac.

Terr. Moll. pl. XLII., fig. 4.

W. G. Binney (Terr. Moll. IV., p. 61) treats this as distinct from *II. hirsuta*, "its characteristics being constant in post-pleiocene fossil as well as in recent individuals." He does not, however, define the characters, and I confess that it is difficult to do so satisfactorily. In *II. stenotrema* the notch is invariably small, and more central than in *II. hirsuta ;* the parietal tooth is more produced over the aperture, and its lower edge is a regular curve, not somewhat sinuous as in the latter and *II. spinosa* Lea; it is also curved downwards at its outer extremity, not terminating abruptly, as usual in those species. The form of the parietal tooth, however, varies in *II. hirsuta*, from which Férussac's species can chiefly, if indeed not alone, be distinguished by the size and position of the notch.

II. stenotrema is not found in the Eastern and Middle States. It does not vary much in size, seldom exceeding,
Diam. maj. 10, min. 9, Alt. 6, mill. Tennessee, Shuttleworth !

Helix spinosa Lea.

This well known species varies in size. Large specimens from Alabama and the Cumberland Mountains, Tenn., are much depressed above and little convex beneath; they measure, Diam. maj. 14, min. 13, Alt. 5 mill.

A small var. from the Look Out Mountains, Tenn. (2000 ft., Bp. Elliott!), is proportionately more elevated above, and more convex at the base, measuring, Diam. maj. 12, min. 11, Alt. 5 mill.

Helix Edgariana Lea.

Plate IV. fig. 18. (Twice nat. size.)

This was described by Lea in the following terms:

CARACOLLA EDGARIANA.

T. supra subplanâ, subtus convexâ, rufo-fuscâ, enormiter striatâ, imperforatâ; spirâ brevi; suturis vix impressis; anfr. 5 planulatis, aperturâ angustissimâ; columellâ dentem unicum longum et laminatum habente; labro incrassato, in medio inciso.

Shell nearly flat above, beneath convex, reddish-brown, irregularly striate, imperforate; spire short; sutures scarcely impressed; whorls 5, flattened; aperture very narrow; columella furnished with a long lamellar tooth; lip thickened, in the middle notched.

Hab.—Cumberland Mountains, Tennessee. Diam. .40, length .20 inch.

Remarks.—Among a number of Helices taken by Mr. Edgar were three specimens of this species, which do not seem to have been before observed. The carina is sharp. The form of the aperture is that of *H. hirsuta* Say, except that the superior and thick part of the lip joins the tooth of the columella; on the surface of the shell there is no hirsute character. Several specimens of the *hirsuta* accompanied them, all of which presented their usual globose character. It differs from *C. spinosa* Nob., in being smaller, less flattened, and being without the cilia. (*Proc. Am. Phil. Soc.,* II. 31. *Trans. Am. Phil. Soc.* IX., p. 2.)

To. Dr. Binney's remarks on *H. spinosa* Lea (Terr. Moll. II., 155), Dr. Gould adds the following:

"There is a small variety of this species, having about half the usual diameter, and having its faces much more convex, which Mr. Lea has described under the name of *Caracolla Edgariana*. Mr. Lea says, its aperture has the form of *H. hirsuta*, except that the superior and thick part of the lip joins the tooth of the columella. We are not yet prepared to admit this as a distinct species, though farther researches may prove it to be so. The junction of the lip with the columellar tooth seems to have been accidental in Mr. Lea's specimens; at least, we have several specimens, corresponding to his in other respects, where this character is wanting. Moreover, there is a large carinated variety of *H. hirsuta*, from the same locality, which, so far as the aperture is concerned, corresponds still better with Mr. Lea's description. His other character, by which he distinguishes *H. Edgariana* from *H. spinosa*, its being without cilia, is not constant, for fresh specimens of both large and small are well garnished with hairs, quite as abundantly as in *H. hirsuta ;* and the difference in the two species is that in the latter the hairs are erect, while in *H. spinosa* they are prostrate. Unfortunately the engravings were made from specimens destitute of hairs."

There are two specimens in my cabinet which accord entirely with Lea's description, and also with fig. 2, Pl. XLIV. Terr. Moll., the habitat of one unknown, the other collected by Bishop Elliott in Tennessee. I have seen no specimen, agreeing otherwise with the type, in which the junction of the lip with the parietal tooth is wanting, and believe it to be a good specific character.

H. Edgariana differs also from *H. spinosa* in the following particulars : it is smaller, more elevated, and more convex beneath. In form the parietal tooth is most like that of *H. stenotrema*, while that of *H. spinosa* is more nearly allied to that usually prevailing in *H. hirsuta*. The whorls of *H. spinosa* are flattened and exserted, the carinated edges of all being seen, but in *H. Edgariana* the upper whorls are rather convex, and defined by a well marked suture. Traces of hairs rarely exist at the base of *H. spinosa*, and no scars indicating their presence are visible on dead or denuded shells, whereas in *H.*

Edgariana there are distant short prostrate hairs, with strongly marked scars on the shell. Fresh or young specimens have no doubt the cilia, as in *H. spinosa.*

The specimen had from Bishop Elliott measures,

Diam. maj. 9, min. 8, Alt. 5 mill.

Helix labrosa nov. sp.

Plate IV., fig. 19, (twice nat. size.)

T. imperforatâ, lenticulari, carinatâ, carinâ pone aperturam subobsoletâ, solidâ, arcuatim striatâ, sub epidermide fusco-corneâ; epidermide tenui, supra setis prostratis munitâ; spirâ convexo-conoideâ, obtusulâ; anf. 5½ planiusculis, ultimo antice deflexo, constricto, basi subinflato, lineis numerosis spiralibus impressis sub epidermide ornato; aperturâ perobliquâ, anguste auriformi, dente valido in toto pariete aperturali linguæformi arcuatim intrante coarctatâ; perist. calloso, reflexiusculo, marginibus callo sinuato junctis, margine basali incrassato, introrsum perdilatato, medio valde inciso.

Shell imperforate, lenticular, carinated, the carina somewhat obsolete behind the aperture, solid, with curved striæ, dark-brown colored beneath the epidermis, thin epidermis with prostrate hairs; spire convex-conoid, obtuse; whorls 5½, rather convex, the last deflexed, constricted, the base inflated, and sculptured beneath the epidermis with numerous impressed spiral lines; the aperture very oblique, narrowly ear-shaped, contracted by a strong linguiform tooth extending along the entire parietal wall; peristome callous, somewhat reflected, the margin joined by a sinuous callus, the basal margin thickened, inwardly much dilated, with a deep and wide notch in the middle.

Diam. maj. 12½, min. 10, Alt. 6½ mill.

Habitat.—Waschita Springs, Arkansas (Cabinet of W. G. Binney); Hot Springs, Arkansas (Cab. Smithsonian Institution); Alabama (W. G. Binney); Tennessee (Bishop Elliott!).

Remarks.—This species has been confounded with *H. Edgariana* Lea, from which, however, it differs in several well marked characters. The specimens to which Mr. W. G. Binney refers (Terr. Moll. IV., p. 65), as being of Lea's species, are of that now under consideration.

The thickened and reflected peristome, and deep wide notch, sufficiently distinguish *H. labrosa* from *H. Edgariana.* The notch in the latter, situated in the centre of the aperture as in *H. stenotrema*, is in a measure obsolete, but in *H. labrosa* it is strongly developed, and nearer to the outer edge of the peristome as in *H. hirsuta.* The form of the parietal tooth of my species is like that of *H. hirsuta*, while *H. Edgariana* is in that particular more like *H. stenotrema.*

H. Edgariana, in fact, connects *H. stenotrema* with *H. spinosa*, but *H. labrosa* is rather allied to *H. hirsuta*, and in the character of the peristome to *H. maxillata* Gould.

W. G. Binney has a pale, thin, apparently immature specimen of *H. labrosa*, entirely agreeing with it as above described, ● excepting that the lower lip is not thickened.

Helix monodon Rackett.

There appears to be no doubt that *H. fraterna* Say is a variety of this species; the degree to which the umbilicus is open is very variable, it is comparatively rarely entirely closed. The parietal tooth is sometimes much elevated, approaching in form to that of *H. hirsuta.* I have several specimens in which the lower lip is continued as in the typical form, so as partially to cover the umbilicus, but in a subsequent stage of growth has its columellar termination duplicated, recurved, and united to the parietal tooth. Occasionally there is a callus, having the appearance of an incipient tooth, on the inner margin of the outer lip.

The following are measurements of specimens in my cabinet.

H. monodon Rack., umbilicus open.

Diam. maj. 11, min. 10, Alt. 5½ mill (6½ whorls), Texas.

"   "   7   "   6   "   4   " (5½   "   ), N. Car.

H. fraterna Say, umbilicus entirely closed.

Diam. maj. 10, min. 9, Alt. 5 mill (5¾ whorls), Goat Isl., N.Y.

"   "   7½   "   6½   "   4   " (5½   "   ), Alabama.

I have three specimens of *H. monodon*, sent to me by Mr. Sloate, formerly of San Francisco, who assured me, on the authority, however, of another person, that they were found near the mouth of the Columbia River, Oregon. I confess that I do not feel satisfied of the correctness of the statement.

H. Leaii Ward is the most striking variety, if not indeed entitled to specific rank; it inhabits by no means so wide an area as *H. monodon* or the var. *H. fraterna*, being found only, I believe, in Michigan, Iowa, Indiana, and Ohio. Mr. Frank Higgins, in his Catalogue of the Mollusca of Columbus, Ohio, insists on its being distinct. He says that it is found in the swamp prairies only, its station being very different to that of *H. monodon*, and that it never appears to extend its range, and does not vary in color of shell or animal.

Mr. A. O. Currier, of Grand Rapids, Michigan, in a late letter remarks, " *H. monodon* and *H. Leaii* have entirely different habits, the former is abundant in dry, the latter rare in moist situations and swamps associated with *Amnicola lapidaria* Say, and other semi-aquatic species. *H. Leaii* lives during half the year under water and ice, while *H. monodon* is found under the bark of trees and rotten stumps. If their stations were changed both would become extinct."

The measurements of my largest and smallest specimens are,

Diam. maj. 8, min. 7, Alt. 4 mill. (5½ whorls), Ohio.

"   "   7   "   6   "   3½   " (5   "   ),   "

Helix appressa Say.

This species is variable in several characters. In Georgia it attains its greatest size; from that State I have examples with

2

six whorls, Diam. maj. 20, min. 18, Alt. 9¼ mill.   Some southern forms are beautifully sculptured with numerous spiral lines, and have a narrow but very projecting parietal tooth.   Near Nashville, Tenn., a small flattened var. is found, widely ribbed above, the ribs obsolete at the base, the lip widely reflected, and the parietal tooth arcuate.

Say's " var. *a*, Labrum with two projecting angles," inhabits Illinois ; in some specimens the aperture and teeth are singularly like those of *H. palliata.*

From Wilmington, N. Car., and City Point, Va., I have a remarkable variety,—depressed, with 4½ whorls, the ribs far apart, and the surface between them somewhat granulated ; the periphery more sharply angulated than in other forms, and the parietal tooth more arcuate.   Diam. maj. 14, min. 11, Alt. 5½ mill.

Specimens from Illinois have the whorls flattened above, and partially exserted, showing a tendency to variation in the same direction as *H. palliata.*

Helix palliata Say.

This shell has been fully identified, but doubts exist as to Say's var. *a.*, *H. obstricta* Say, *H. helicoides* Lea, and *H. Carolinensis* Lea.   Having had much correspondence with conchologists, both here and in Europe, respecting those forms, I propose fully to examine the questions which have arisen concerning them.

In 1821 Say thus described *H. palliata* and *H. obstricta*, (*Jour. Acad. Nat. Sci., Phila.* II., *pp.* 152–154),—

H. PALLIATA.—Shell depressed, with elevated lines, forming grooves between them ; epidermis fuscous, rugose with very numerous minute tuberculous acute prominences ; volutions five, depressed above, beneath rounded, forming an obtuse angle exteriorly, which is more acute near the termination of the labrum ; umbilicus covered with a white callus ; aperture contracted by the labrum ; labrum widely reflected, with two profound obtuse sinuses on the inner side above the middle, forming a prominent distinct tooth between them, and a projecting angle near the middle of the lip; labium with a large, prominent white tooth, placed perpendicularly to the whorl, and obliquely to the axis of the shell, and nearly attaining the umbilical callus.

Inhabits Illinois. Length of the column seven-twentieths of an inch. Greatest breadth, four-fifths of an inch.

Var. *a.*—A very prominent acute carina, destitute of minute prominences. Inhabits Ohio. Breadth nearly one inch.

H. OBSTRICTA.—Shell depressed, with elevated lines forming grooves between them; epidermis pale-brownish, naked; volutions five, depressed above, beneath rounded, with an acute, projecting carina; umbilicus covered with a white callus, indented; mouth resembling that of *H. palliata.*

Inhabits Ohio. Breadth nearly one inch.

This species is very closely allied to *H. palliata*, but the epidermis is not covered with small elevations as in that shell, and the carina is very prominent and remarkable.

In 1831 Lea described the following species :

H. CAROLINENSIS.—T. supradepressâ, infra inflatâ, oblique striatâ, fuscâ, imperforatâ; anfr. 5, spirâ maxime obtusâ; aperturâ coarctatâ; labro albo, reflexo, latoque, duobus dentibus instructo, quorum inferior longus et laminatus, superior parvus et conicus est, columellâ dentem elevatum incurvumque habente, columellæ basi valde impressâ. Diam. $\frac{11}{20}$ths. Length $\frac{7}{20}$ths inch.

Hab.—South Carolina, near Cheraw.

Shell depressed above, inflated below, obliquely striated, fuscous, imperforate; whorls 5; spire very obtuse; aperture contracted; outer lip white, broad, and reflected, furnished with two teeth, the inferior one long and lamellar, the superior one small and conical; columella with an elevated incurved tooth; base of the columella much impressed.

Remarks.—I found a few specimens of this fine Helix while travelling through South Carolina three years since. They were taken from beneath the bark of an old tree. It is closely allied to Mr. Say's *palliata*, but differs in the region of the base of the columella being more deeply impressed. The oblique striæ are more distinct, and no specimen which I obtained is in the least hirsute. (*Trans. Amer. Phil. Soc., N. S. IV., p.* 108, *Pl.* XV., *figs.* 33–a. b. c.)

CARACOLLA HELICOIDES.—T. orbiculatâ, fuscâ, supra plano-convexâ, subtus inflatâ, imperforatâ, oblique striatâ; anfr. 5, spirâ obtusissimâ; aperturâ contractâ; labro albo, lato et reflexo, dentibus duobus instructo, quorum inferior longus et laminatus, superior parvus et conicus est; columellâ dentem unicum, longum, elevatum et incurvum habente. Diam. ⅛⅓ths. Length ₂₀⁹₀ths inch.

Hab.—Tennessee, near Nashville.

II. palliata? Say var. a. *Acad. Nat. Soc.* II., *p.* 152.

Shell orbicular, fuscous, plano-convex above, inflated below, imperforate, obliquely striated; whorls 5; spire very obtuse; aperture contracted; outer lip white, broad, and reflected, furnished with two teeth, the inferior one long and lamellar, the superior one small and conical; columella with a long, elevated, incurved tooth.

Remarks.—Among the fine shells brought by Prof. Vanuxem, some years since, from a tour through the Western States, were two specimens of this beautiful Caracolla. In its specific characters it resembles *II. palliata* Say, and *II. Carolinensis* described in this paper. It is destitute of the hirsute appearance of the *palliata*, and is entirely distinct in the flatness of the whorls of the spire. In the *Carolinensis* the base of the columella is more impressed, and the whorls more inflated. (*Trans. Amer. Phil. Soc. l. c., p.* 109, *Pl.* XV., *figs.* 34, *a, b, c.*)

On the cover of No. 6, of his American Conchology (1834), Say published the following note:

C. helicoides Lea, Trans. Am. Phil. Soc., IV. N. S., is var. *a.* of *H. palliata* Say, *H. denotata* Fer.

H. Carolinensis Ibid. corresponds by description and figures with *H. appressa* Say, var. *a.*

Dr. Binney, in the Boston Journal (1840), and also in the Terr. Moll. (1851), places *II. obstricta* and Lea's two species in the synonymy of *II. palliata.* W. G. Binney (Terr. Moll. IV., 1859) observes that the extreme variation of *II. palliata* has given rise to considerable confusion. He designates *II. Carolinensis* as "a prominent variety," but holds *II. obstricta* to be distinct, having no doubt of its identity with *II. helicoides;* he adds to the synonymy of *H. obstricta* Say's var. *a.* of *H. palliata*, considering that the descriptions agree. The name *H. denotata* appears in Férussac's Prodromus. In the Histoire, Pl. 50, fig. 7, agrees with Lea's figure of *H. helicoides*, but in the Explication des Planches it is erroneously called *H. appressa* Say. In the Bull. Zool. (1835), Férussac refers *H. Carolinensis* to *H. palliata*, and treats *H. helicoides* as a variety of it. Pfeiffer (Mon. Hel. Viv.) has *H. Carolinensis* in the synonymy of *H. palliata*, and *H. helicoides* in that of *H. obstricta*.

I have now quoted everything of any moment which has been written on the subject of the different forms of, or immediately allied to *H. palliata*.

There can be no doubt as to the *H. palliata* Say. It is impossible, however, with absolute certainty to identify Say's var. *a.* and his *H. obstricta*, looking at the descriptions, and his note of 1834 on *H. helicoides*. Say gives Ohio as the habitat of the two first, which increases the difficulty, inasmuch as no carinated form, so far as I know, occurs in that State.

Say, in 1824, separated *H. obstricta* from var. *a.* ; in 1834 he pronounced *H. helicoides* to be the latter, and did not mention the former. At the latter date he erroneously referred *H. Carolinensis* to *H. appressa*, and I believe that he was equally in error in referring *H. helicoides* to var. *a.* instead of to *H. obstricta*.

Judging alone from Say's diagnosis of *H. obstricta*, I should certainly consider it identical with *H. helicoides* as *figured* by Lea, who, in his description, makes no allusion to the carina. Say characterizes the carina of *H. obstricta* as *acute, projecting, very prominent, and remarkable*. In *H. helicoides* the carina is certainly remarkable; projecting from the edges of all save the apicial whorls, compressed, and overlapping the suture, as in *H. Cumberlandiana* Lea, a shell unknown to Say. Under these circumstances I concur with W. G. Binney in placing *H. helicoides* in the synonymy of *H. obstricta*.

H. palliata, var. *a.*, is described by Say as having a very prominent acute carina, and destitute of minute prominences.

The only shell to which the description applies (excluding *H. obstricta*) is *H. Carolinensis* or an intermediate form, and I am decidedly of opinion that Lea's species has been misunderstood by authors; that it is in fact a variety of *H. obstricta*, to which it is nearly allied in epidermis and sculpturing, rather than of *H. palliata*, from which, in those particulars, it essentially differs.

The nature of the epidermis and sculpturing are the only constant specific characters which distinguish *H. palliata* from *H. obstricta*. In the former the epidermis has " numerous minute tuberculous acute prominences;" the striæ are close together, and somewhat irregular in development. In the typical form the whorls are convex, with a well impressed suture ; the last whorl is obtusely angulated in front of, but not behind the aperture.

The following are the dimensions of the largest and smallest specimens in my cabinet.

Diam. maj. 23, min. 20, Alt. 10 mill. (5 whorls).
"   "   17 "   14 "   8 "   (4½ ").

The species varies in the form of the whorls and extent of the angulation of the periphery, as follows.

VAR. β.—Whorls flattened above, slightly exserted, the last more sharply angulated in front of the aperture, with the striæ, especially behind the aperture, more distinctly defined.

Diam. maj. 22, min. 19½, Alt. 8½ mill. (5 whorls).

I am indebted to Mr. A. O. Currier of Grand Rapids, Mich., for beautiful specimens from Mumfordsville, Ky., and Pittsburg Landing, Tenn.

VAR. γ.—Whorls planulate above, and so exserted as to show the carinated edges of all excepting the apicial whorls, the last whorl with an acute projecting carina continued to the back of the aperture ; the umbilicus not always entirely covered by the reflected lip.

Diam. maj. 21½, min. 18½, Alt. 7 mill. (5 whorls).

Bishop Elliott collected fine specimens at Jasper Town, Tenn.

Helix obstricta Say.

SYNONYMY.

Helix *obstricta Say* Jour. Acad. Nat. Sci. Phila., II., 154, 1821.
—— *palliata Say var. a.* Jour. Acad., l. c., 152.
—— *Carolinensis Lea* Trans. Amer. Phil. Soc. N. S., IV.,
108, pl. XV., figs. 33, a, b, c, 1831.
Caracolla *helicoides Lea* Trans Amer. Phil. Soc., l. c., 109,
pl. XV., figs. 34, a, b, c.
Helix *palliata Binney* Terr. Moll. II., 136, var. pl. XV., 1851.
—— —— *var. H. Carolinensis W. G. Binney.* Terr.
Moll. IV., 57, 1859.

From the dates at which this species and its varieties were
described, the most distinctly carinated form must be treated
as the type, although the nature of the variations is the same
as in *H. palliata.*

H. obstricta Say (*H. helicoides* Lea) differs from *H. palliata*
in the following particulars ; the epidermis is free from "tuberculous prominences," but has raised spiral lines between the
costæ on the upper and lower surfaces of the shell. It has elevated, rigid, distant costæ, the whorls are subexserted and
acutely carinated, the carina of the upper whorls compressed,
and overlapping the sutures as in *H. Cumberlandiana* Lea.
The umbilicus, as in the most carinated form of *H. palliata,* is
not always entirely covered by the reflected lip.

The typical form varies in color from pale to dark brown,
and also in size and elevation, as the following measurements
will show :

Diam. maj. 25, min. 22, Alt. 10 mill. (5½ whorls). Cab. W.
G. Binney, Lea ! ·
"   " 23 " 20 " 8½ " (5 whorls). Bersh. Spr.,
Tenn., Elliott! My Cab.
"   " 20 " 17½ " 8 " (5 whorls). Indiana, Dr.
Ingalls ! My Cab.

VAR. β. Whorls subexserted, carina less acute and prominent, partially obsolete behind the aperture, not covering the sutures.

Diam. maj. 24, min. 19, Alt. 8 mill. (5 whorls).

"   "   20½ "   17 "   7 "   (5   "   ).

Bp. Elliott collected many specimens at Columbus, Geo. This var connects *H. Carolinensis* Lea with *H. obstricta*, and is generally found in cabinets under the former name.

VAR. γ. Whorls more convex, the last obtusely angulated in front of, but very little behind the aperture.

Diam. maj. 21, min. 17, Alt. 7½ mill. (5 whorls). South Carolina, Lea! Cab. Acad. Nat. Sci. Phila.

Diam maj. 18, min. 16, Alt. 7 mill. (5 whorls). My Cabinet.

This is the typical *H. Carolinensis* Lea, holding precisely the same relation to *H. obstricta*, as *H. palliata* to *H. palliata* var. γ.

Helix vultuosa Gould.

Pl. IV. fig. 21.

I have lately received from Mr. A. O. Currier, of Grand Rapids, Michigan, a very instructive specimen collected near Pine Town, Cherokee County, Texas, by Miss S. N. Bates.

It is larger than the usual form, and has the characteristics of the species singularly developed. The last whorl is so produced as to leave both the lip teeth far within the aperture; the exterior *scrobiculi* are long and deep, the space between them being almost as much elevated as in *H. auriculata* Say.

In specimens had from Dr. Gould, the edge of the peristome between the teeth is thickened, but in the example before me it is produced into an erect, white, polished lamella, 3 mill. long and 1½ mill. in height, as shown in my figure.

Dr. Gould remarks, that *H. vultuosa* differs from *H. Texasiana* Mor., " by having no line of callus connecting the pillartooth with the angle of the lip, thereby forming a re-entering

angle." There is, however, a callus at the lower termination of
the pillar-tooth, extending nearly 1 mill. in the direction of the
upper angle of the lip, which is shown in the figure of the aperture, Terr. Moll. III., pl. XL. In Mr. Currier's specimen this
callus extends for a short distance across the parietal wall, at a
right angle with the tooth, and is thence continued upwards
towards, but not so far as the upper angle of the lip.

I subjoin measurements—

Diam. maj. 10, min. 9, Alt. 5½ mill.   Dr. Gould's specimen.
  "   "   12   "   10½ "   6   "   A. O. Currier's "

It is curious to notice how much the increased development
of the characters of *H. vultuosa* gives to that species affinities,
not existing in the typical form, with the group to which *H.
auriculata* belongs.

But I should remark that some of the North American Helices, especially the toothed species, are by intermediate varieties
connected in a marked degree.

Note on the Toothed Helices of North America.

The frequent occurrence of toothed shells of the Genus Helix
on the North American Continent is very remarkable.

In W. G. Binney's " Check List" of the species of " Eastern
North America from the boreal regions to the Rio Grande,"
published by the Smithsonian Institution, 116 are enumerated,
of which no less than 61 have one or more teeth in the aperture,
or within the whorls.   In his list of the species of the " Pacific
Coast from the extreme north to Mazatlan," Binney mentions
31 species, of which four have teeth, while 8 have them out of
31 named (exclusive of those embraced in the Pacific Coast
list), in his list of Mexican Helices.   Species similarly armed
are numerous in the West Indies, and not unfrequent in Central and parts of South America.

What office in the economy of the living tenants of the shells
these processes, showing much uniformity of design, are des-

tined to perform, it is difficult, indeed impossible, in the present state of our knowledge, to comprehend. When the teeth, from their form and number, contract to a considerable degree the apertural space through which the animal can alone protrude itself, they appear capable of affording to it protection against the entry of its enemies, or a means of removing particles of earth or other foreign matter adhering to its mucous-covered body, when withdrawing into its habitation. I am not, however, aware of any differences in the habits of the animals of shells with and without teeth, which warrant such or any other theories as to their value. Shells with large and small, toothed and toothless apertures, are found inhabiting the same localities, and subject to the same external influences and circumstances.

The form and position, and with very trifling exceptions the number of the teeth, are constant and reliable specific characters. In proof of this, and as evidence of their value, I may mention that when the aperture of a toothed shell is accidentally broken, the animal not only repairs the injured part, but reproduces the teeth. I have specimens of *H. appressa*, *inflecta*, *monodon*, *septemvolva*, and *tridentata*, in which, after the formation of the parietal tooth, the aperture and part of the last whorl adjoining were broken off, and the animals not only reconstructed the reflected lips of their shells, but added also the parietal teeth, the old ones remaining as monuments of the destroyed apertures. In one of my specimens of *H. tridentata*, after completion of the shell, the animal continued the last whorl about 2 mill. beyond the lip, partially reflected the new lip, and added two incipient teeth in advance of the old ones. On Plate IV., fig. 20, a sketch is given of the very singular reparation of one of my specimens of *H. septemvolva*. The fracture was behind the aperture, which the animal in consequence abandoned, but it formed a new one by reflecting the outer lip, on the lower part of which it added a small tooth,—it found insufficient space for another parietal tooth behind the old aperture.

A number of the North American Helices have, besides the teeth, the process first noticed by Lea (Obs. V., 60), as a "pillar or additional column, placed like a fulcrum (buttress) in the interior, against the wall of the ordinary column, at the distance of a fifth to a third of a revolution of the whorl from the aperture." Lea first observed this in *II. spinosa*, and subsequently in seven other species. He remarks that the fulcrum "will be found in some species to be a simple round column soldered to the paries of the main column; in others a compressed or flattened column extending into the cavity of the whorl." The purpose, he adds, "of this fulcrum or buttress is very evidently instituted for the greater strength of the ultimate whorl, which, being very much enlarged, seems in some of these more delicate species to require additional support."

With regard to the particular use of this curious appendage, which exists only, so far as I know, in shells having the aperture contracted by teeth, I suggest that it acts literally as a *fulcrum*, in connexion with which the muscles of the animal have increased leverage power to draw back its protruded body into the shell, in the performance of which operation the teeth are obstacles,—yet many toothed shells are without this process.

In repaired individuals of *II. monodon*, not only is a new parietal tooth added, as above mentioned, but the *fulcrum* is also reconstructed in its proper position with respect to the new aperture. The locality of the old fulcrum is indicated by a callus,— whether it was broken off or removed by the animal I am unable to determine.

The following, framed from personal observation of specimens in my cabinet, presents an arrangement of the species of Helix of Eastern North America, based on the number of teeth, distinguishing those which have the fulcrum, and also the character of the lip—whether simple or reflected.

A. LIP SIMPLE—NO FULCRUM.
   1. *One tooth within at base of aperture.*
      II. perspectiva Say.

2. *Two teeth within at base of aperture.*
  H. suppressa Say.
  " gularis   "
3. *Two internal lamellæ.*
  H. lasmodon Phill.
4. *Two or more internal teeth repeated in two or more series.*
  H. lineata Say.
  " interna   "

  ―

  " multidentata By.

B. LIP REFLECTED—NO FULCRUM.
  5. *One parietal tooth.**
    H. exoleta By.
    " thyroides Say.
    " bucculenta Gould.
    " Wheatleyi Bland.
    " dentifera By.
    " Roemeri Pfr.

    ―

    " Christyi Bland—allied in form to H. inflecta Say.
  6. *One tooth on lower lip.†*
    H. profunda Say.

    ―

    " Pennsylvanica Green, tooth not prominently developed.
  7. *One parietal tooth, and one on lower lip.*
    H. Sayii By.
  8. *One parietal tooth, and one (lamelliform) on lower lip.*
    H. elevata Say—var. without lip tooth.
    " Clarkii Lea.
    " appressa Say—var. with outer lip tooth, like *H. palliata.*
  9. *One parietal tooth, one (lamelliform) on lower lip and one on outer lip.*
    H. palliata Say.
    " obstricta "

* *H. albolabris* not unfrequently, and *H. multilineata* rarely have this tooth.

† *H. albolabris, exoleta,* and *thyroides* have often a tooth-like callus on the lower lip near its columellar termination.

10. *One parietal and two lip teeth.*
   H. inflecta Say.
   " Rugeli Shuttl.

   ———

   " tridentata Say.
   " Hopetonensis Shuttl.
   " fallax Say.

11. *One parietal lamella, continued from its lower end upwards to superior termination of lip, and two lip teeth.*
   H. triodontoides Bland.
   " Hindsi Pfr.   } upper lip tooth modification of the notch of
   " ventrosula Pfr. }   *H. hirsuta.*
   " Texasiana Mor.—both lip teeth ditto.

12. *Modification of same form of parietal lamella, with no lip teeth.*
   H. septemvolva Say.

   ———

   " cereolus Muhlf.   } have also an internal lamina.
   " Carpenteriana Bland. }

13. *Modification of same form of parietal lamella, with two lip teeth, more or less lamelliform.*
   H. oppilata Mor.
   " auriformis Bland, upper lip tooth with incipient hook.

   " avara Say.
   " espiloca Rav.   } upper lip tooth with hook; the lip
   " Postelliana Bland. } teeth especially in *H. auriformis* and
   " auriculata Say. } *H. avara* are modifications of the
   " uvulifera Shuttl. } notch of *H. hirsuta.*

   " Ariadne Pfr.

14. *Two parallel parietal laminæ, with internal teeth.*
   H. labyrinthica Say.

   ———

   H. Hubbardi Brown.*

C. With fulcrum.
   15. *One parietal lamelliform tooth, lower lip more or less laminated.*

* The lip of *H. Hubbardi* is reflected. Brown in his description (Proc. Acad. N. Sci., Phila. 1861), by an oversight has the word " simplici" as well as " breviter reflexo."

H. monodon Rack., lip reflected, var. with denticle on outer lip.

" barbigera Redf.   "

—

H. Edvardsi Bland, small notch, lower lip more or less appressed.

" spinosa Lea,   "   "   "

—

. H. Edgariana Lea,   "   "   "

" stenotrema Fer.,   "   "   "

—

H. hirsuta Say, deep notch,   "   "

" labrosa Bland,   "   lower lip produced.

—

H. maxillata Gould, no notch, lower lip produced and duplicated within the aperture.

D.   LIP REFLECTED—WITH FULCRUM.

16. *Parietal process modification of* § 11, *and two lip teeth.*

H. leporina Gould—lip teeth modified form of notch.

" pustuloides Bland.

" pustula Fer.

—

H. Mooreana W G. By.

" tholus.*   "

—

H. vultuosa Gould, continuation of parietal lamella to lip incipient only.

—

H. Dorfeuilliana Lea.

" Troostiana   "

" fastigans L. W. Say.

" Hazardi Bland.

17. *One parietal and two lip teeth.*

H. introferens Bland,—allied to *H. fallax* and *H. vultuosa.*

18. *Parietal process modification of* § 11, *with lamella on lower lip and two extending downwards, forming, far within the aperture, a modified duplication of the lower lip, with notch having reflexed hook.*

H. hippocrepis Pfr.

* *H. tholus* is, I believe, a large var. of *H. Mooreana.*

The four species having teeth, comprised in W. G. Binney's Pacific Coast List, are *H. germana* Gould, allied to *H. monodon* Rack., but without the fulcrum, belonging to the foregoing section 5; *H. devia* Gould, to section 8; *H. acutedentata* W. G. By., to 13, assuming from its affinity with *H. Ariadne* that it has no fulcrum, and *H. loricata* Gould, which has a well developed tubercle, belonging to section 17. To these may be added *H. Mullani* Bland and Cooper (sec. 9), and *H. polygyrella* Bld. and Coop., which, unlike any other North American species, has, with an unreflected lip, a parietal tooth and two series of three teeth in each within the last whorl.

Note on Variation in Species of Helix in Eastern North America.

It will be seen from the foregoing remarks that many of the species of Helix inhabiting Eastern North America are subject to considerable variation. Without entering upon the question of causes of variation, I should notice that, with the exception of size, the variability of shells is rather in ornamentation than in characters which indicate differences in the structure of the animals, or can affect their welfare.

The variations referred to are chiefly in size, color, sculpture, and degree of the angulation of the periphery.

Wollaston (On the Variation of Species, p. 106) refers to the tendency exhibited by many Helices to have at least two abruptly marked forms, a larger and a smaller one. He says— "I have indeed been shown specimens by Sir Chas. Lyell of the *H. hirsuta* Say from N. America, one state of which is considerably more than double the dimensions of the other; and I believe it is a well known fact that intermediate links have not yet been observed to connect the extremes." So far, however, as my experience teaches, I must say that, without exception, the extremes in N. American Helices are connected by others of intermediate sizes.

The tendency of species, in different groups of the same genus, to vary as regards form in a similar direction, is certainly curious. *H. palliata* Say, with whorls convex above, and an obsoletely angulated periphery, has a variety with flattened, sub-exserted whorls, and carinated periphery. The same differences exist between *H. Carolinensis* Lea and *H obstricta* Say, and although in a less degree in forms of *H. appressa* Say. There is also the same relation between *H. hirsuta* Say and *H spinosa* Lea, and I may add between *H. Troostiana* Lea and *H. fastigans* L. W. Say.

In the species without teeth there appears to be less tendency to carination,—but *H. Cumberlandiana* Lea has the same relation to *H. alternata* Say as *H. obstricta* to *H. palliata.* There is also a carinated variety of *H. intertexta* Binney.

It is worthy of remark that the *striæ* in *H. alternata* and *H. palliata* are replaced by *costæ* in *H. Cumberlandiana* and *obstricta.*

The geographical distribution of the carinated forms above mentioned is interesting. None are found in the Eastern or Middle States ; they inhabit chiefly Kentucky, Tennessee, Alabama, and Georgia,—Tennessee being their metropolis.

Darwin (Origin of Species, p. 143, Amer. Ed.) states the following propositions,—" distinct species present analogous variations ; and a variety of one species often assumes some of the characters of an allied species, or reverts to some of the characters of an early progenitor." He gives as a case of analogous variation in the vegetable kingdom, the enlarged stems of the common turnip, Swedish turnip, and Rutabaga, remarking that, " according to the ordinary view of each species having been independently created, we should have to attribute this similarity in the enlarged stems of these three plants, not to the *vera causa* of community of descent, and a consequent tendency to vary in a like manner, but to three separate yet closely related acts of creation." I certainly am not prepared to accept community of descent as the cause of analogous variation in the American Helices above mentioned.

In connexion with the subject of variation, I may refer to the great length of time during which species have been perpetuated without alteration. In the Post-pleiocene beds of the Southern States a considerable number of the Helices and other land, and also fresh water species, occur identical with those now living. *H. labyrinthica* Say, widely distributed in North America, is said to be an Eocene fossil in England.

When species have well defined colors, or colored bands, or other ornamentation, uniformly pale individuals are usually noticed as varieties. I have such, in my cabinet, of the following Helices, viz.: *alternata, solitaria, albolabris, multilineata, perspectiva, thyroides, interna, profunda, Pennsylvanica, palliata, inflecta, tridentata, fallax,* and *hirsuta.*

In North America there is no species of Helix which, in its normal state, is *sinistral,* but I may record that I have reversed *H. alternata, thyroides,* and *Mitchelliana;* W. G. Binney has *H. fallax,* Mr. Isaac Lea *H. hirsuta,* and Mr. Anthony, I believe, *H. inflecta* and *H. solitaria.*

LIST OF FIGURES ON PLATE IV.

3

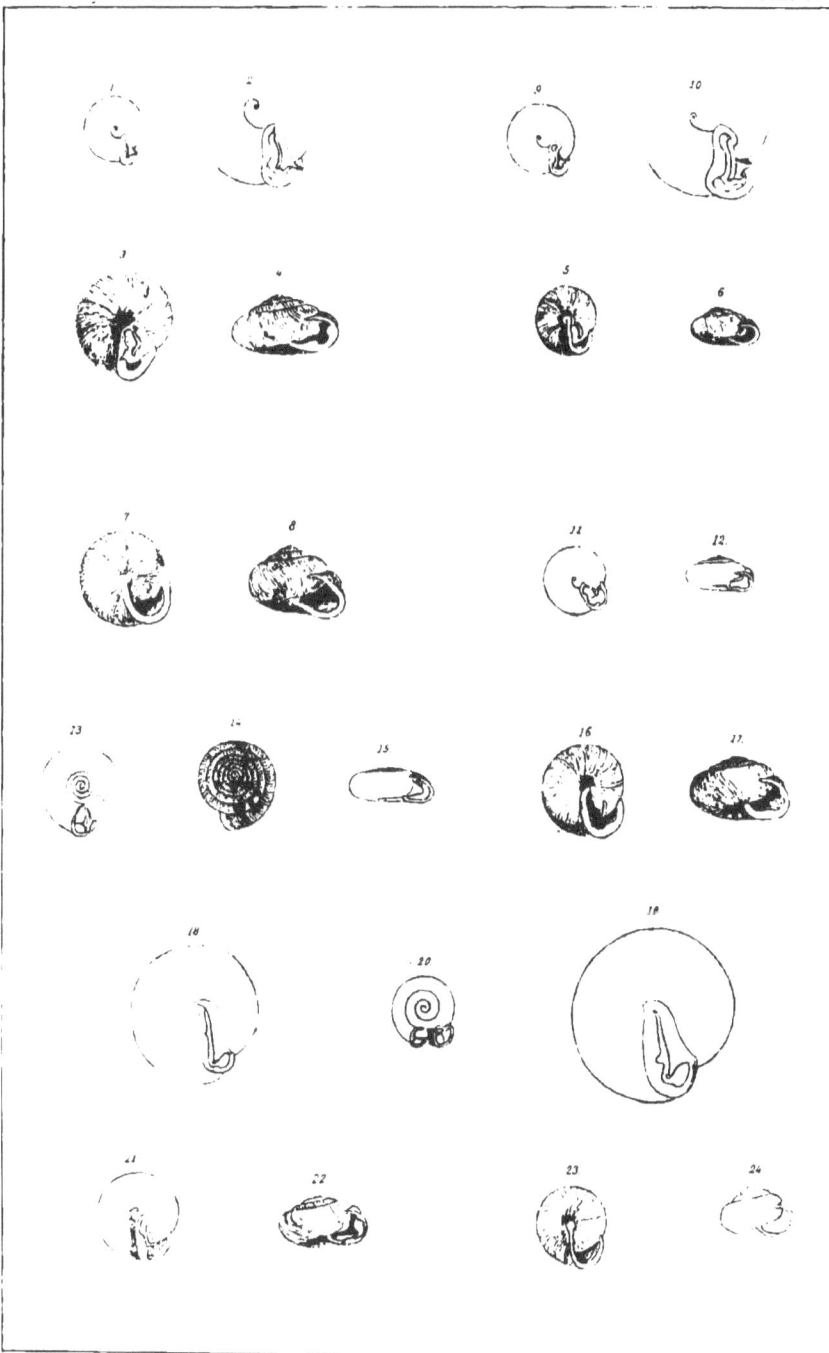

Notice of Land and Freshwater Shells collected by Dr. J. G. Cooper in the Rocky Mountains, etc., in 1860.

BY T. BLAND AND J. G. COOPER.

Read June 17, 1861.

Reprinted from the Annals of the Lyceum of Natural History, New York, Vol. VII., June, 1861.

THE shells, which form the subject of this paper, were collected by Dr. J. G. Cooper, during the progress of a military expedition under the command of Major Blake, U.S.A. The party went from St. Louis in the Spring of 1860 by steamboat to Fort Benton, crossed over the mountains from that point to the waters of the Columbia River, where it again embarked, and proceeded to the Pacific Coast.

Dr. Cooper forwarded his notes and specimens to Mr. W. Cooper, who placed them in the hands of Mr. T. Bland with a view to the preparation of the subjoined notice.

Helix Townsendiana Lea, Trans. Amer. Phil. Soc., vi. 99, pl. 23, f. 80.

This species was brought by Mr. Nuttall, Dr. Townsend, and the United States Exploring Expedition from the neighborhood of the Wahlamat, near its junction with the Columbia River. Dr. Cooper collected many examples, varying much in size, but none so large as those which we have seen from Oregon.

The following is a copy of his note on the specimens,—" The numerous small specimens were found in the dry prairie at the junction of Hell Gate and Bitter Root Rivers, and as I met with larger ones of various sizes in more damp situations of the woods, from an elevation of 4800 feet down to 2200 feet, at the base of the Bitter Root Range, I presume that the former is a dwarfed variety, such as is found also west of the Coast Mountains in Washington Territory. This is the most wide-spread species I have seen." Other specimens forwarded by Dr.

Cooper are labelled, " both slopes of the Bitter Root Mountains from 5600 feet to 2200 feet."

In Binney's Terr. Moll. II. 162, the greatest transverse diameter of Oregon examples, is said to be 1⅜ inch.

The following are the measurements of large and small specimens from Dr. Cooper's shells.

Diam. maj. 23, min. 20, Alt. 13 mil.
 "   "   17, "   13½, "   9 "

The small variety is generally more strongly and coarsely wrinkled.

Dr. Cooper in the Pacific R. R. Report, gives Puget's Sound, W. T., as a habitat of this species,—it has also been found at Cape Disappointment, on the borders of Oregon and Washington Territory.

Helix Mullani, nov. sp.

T. subobtecte-umbilicatâ, globoso-depressâ, fusco-corneâ, irregulariter striatâ, epidermide tenui, sub lente lineis spiralibus, et tuberculis (setos gerentibus?) munitâ, sub epidermide nitidâ; spirâ brevi; anfr. 5½–6 convexis, ultimo antice gibbo, vix descendente, basi læviusculo, ad aperturam valde constricto; aperturâ subtriangulari, obliquâ, dente brevi, albo, linguiformi, in pariete aperturali intrante subcoarctatâ; perist. albo, vel rufo-corneo, expanso, fornicatim reflexo, bidentato, dentibus duobus albis in margine calli positis, 1 inferiore lamelliformi, altero, sæpe obsoleto, parvo; margine columellari umbilicum mediocrem pervium semioccultante.

Shell with umbilicus partially covered, globose-depressed, dark horn colored, irregularly striated, having a thin epidermis with microscopic spiral lines, and tubercles (the latter with hairs?); beneath the epidermis shining; spire short; whorls 5½ to 6, convex, the last gibbous above, scarcely descending, the base rather smooth, much constricted at the aperture; aperture subtriangular, oblique, with a short white linguiform parietal tooth; peristome white, or reddish horn colored, thickened, expanded, and roundly reflected, with two teeth on the margin of the callus, the lower one lamelliform, the other small, often obsolete, the columellar margin partially covering the middling sized pervious umbilicus.

Diam. maj. 13½, min. 11, Alt. 7 mill.

Station.—Under logs and in dry pine woods.

Habitat.—Dead specimens found near Coeur d'Alêne Mission, Coeur d'Alêne Mountains;—living ones on the west side , of the Bitter Root Mountains, Washington Territory, J. G. Cooper!; St. Joseph's River, 1st Camp, Oregon, Cabinet of W. G. Binney.

Remarks.—This species is most nearly allied in form to *H. Columbiana* Lea* (*H. labiosa* Gould), the peristome is however not only more thickened, but also singularly reflected behind the plane of the aperture, producing a canal behind it, leading from the upper margin into the umbilicus. Being tridentate it has some alliance with *H. tridentata* Say, but that shell is of coarser texture, more depressed, has a more open umbilicus, and the form of the peristome and teeth are different.

Dr. Cooper found a beautiful hyaline specimen under a stone " by the Bitter Root River, at an elevation of 4000 feet, on a hill called ' Half Way ' 30 miles below the junction." This variety is much depressed, translucent, delicately striated, and has the parietal tooth only. The very thin epidermis shows the spiral lines, and the last whorl numerous scars of the tubercles mentioned in our description of the species. In Mr. Binney's specimen from Oregon the umbilicus is wider, and not so much covered by the peristome as in the other examples.

The species is named in honor of Lieutenant Mullan, U.S.A., who has done much in collecting the natural products of the region in which it was found.

---

* A specimen of *H. Columbiana* Lea in the Cabinet of T. Bland, has a well developed parietal tooth, the same as in *H. thyroides* Say.

Helix polygyrella, nov. sp.

T. late umbilicatâ, discoideâ, planulatâ, nitidâ, translucidâ, luteo-corneâ, superne costulatâ, costis ad aperturam obsoletis, basi læviusculâ, spirâ vix elevatâ ; anfr. 7–8 convexiusculis, lente accrescentibus, ultimo antice breviter deflexo, intus seriebus duobus remotis trium dentium munito ; umbilico ad apicem pervio ; aperturâ subverticali, obliquâ, lunato-ovali ; perist. superne depresso, albo, simplici, valde incrassato, marginibus dente pliciformi, elevato, albo, triangulari junctis.

Shell widely umbilicate, discoidal, flat, shining, translucent, yellowish horn colored, ribbed above, the ribs obsolete near the aperture, base rather smooth ; spire scarcely elevated ; whorls 7-8, somewhat convex, gradually increasing, the last slightly deflexed above, armed within with two rows of three teeth, seen through the outer wall ; umbilicus pervious, of equal size to the apex ; aperture subvertical, oblique, lunate-oval ; peristome depressed above, white, simple, much thickened within, the margins joined by a white pliciform elevated triangular tooth.

Diam. maj. 11½, min. 10¼, Alt. 5 mill.

Station.—Inhabits moss and decaying wood in the dampest parts of the spruce forests.

Habitat.—Common on the Cœur d'Alêne Mountains, especially on their eastern slope.   J. G. Cooper!

Remarks.—This very interesting species is unlike any shell, with which we are acquainted, hitherto found on the North American Continent.   Although entirely distinct from the Brazilian *H. polygyrata* Born it has some affinity with it, especially as regards the form generally, and the presence of the internal teeth. *H. polygyrata* has five teeth within the last whorl, three on the under surface of the outer wall, and two opposite to the others on the exterior of the penultimate whorl.   Our species has two distinct rows of three teeth, all the teeth being on the

under surface of the outer whorl; the first row nearly opposite
to the aperture, the second between the first and the parietal
tooth; in one specimen, the second row is immediately behind
that tooth, and visible through the shell just within the
aperture.

Helix Vancouverensis Lea Trans. Amer. Phil. Soc. vi., 87, pl.
23, f. 72.

Mr. Isaac Lea described this from specimens brought by
Mr. Nuttall from the banks of the Columbia River, Oregon.
In 1840, Dr. Binney (Bost. Jl. iii. 372) considered it the same
as *H. concava* Say, although he afterwards (Terr. Moll. ii. 166),
in deference to the opinions of others, treated it as distinct.
The two are certainly *very* closely allied. Dr. Gould described
*H. sportella** (Bost. Proc. ii. 167) in 1846; it was brought by
the U. S. Exploring Expedition from Puget Sound, Oregon.
Gould's differs from Lea's species in having the incremental
striæ more or less decussated by revolving lines, giving it a
granulated appearance. In some individuals the decussation
is to a great extent obsolete, or confined to the upper whorls
only, and it seems to us that the two species cannot be separated. The same differences prevail in forms of the Cuban *H.*
Sagemon Beck. *H. vellicata* Forbes is certainly identical with
Lea's species.

H. Vancouverensis has a wide distribution. Dr. Cooper collected it "on the west side of the Coeur d'Alêne Mountains, W.T.
in the forests of Coniferæ, &c., such as it inhabits west of the
Cascade range." He remarks, "there is a wide plain between
those two ranges quite uninhabitable by Helices on account of
drought, for a distance of about two hundred miles, but this
species and *H. Townsendiana Lea* probably extend round its
north end through the forests near lat. 49° N." We have
it from the vicinity of Crescent City, California (Dr. W.

* In form and sculpture *H. sportella* is curiously allied to *H. euspira* Pfr. from
Venezuela.

Newcomb!), also from Oregon City, and Whidby's Island, W. T.

It is found on the Pacific coast from Puget Sound to San Diego, Lower California.

Helix strigosa Gould Proc. Bost. Soc. N. II. ii. 166.

This species was brought by the U. S. Exploring Expedition from the interior of Oregon.

Dr. Cooper found it in Washington Territory " on the Rocky Mountains by the Bitter Root River, at an elevation of 4000 feet, æstivating under logs of pine, on a steep slope of shale containing lime in veins."

The shells collected by Dr. Cooper are of smaller dimensions than those given by Gould, the former measure diam. maj. 19, min. 17, alt. 7 mill. The outer whorl is more carinated, with a more distinct reddish brown band above, and also below the periphery. In some the penultimate whorl shows at the suture its acutely carinated edge, excavated near the margin, and with an impressed line, as in *H. Cumberlandiana* Lea. The somewhat distant spiral lines at the base, intersecting the incremental striæ, produce a semi-granulated appearance. In old examples the margins of the peristome are joined by a parietal callous deposit.

This species also occurs in the Big Horn Mountains, in Nebraska, and on the Rio Piedra, in W. New Mexico.

One specimen reached us with the animal alive ; kept in a glass vessel with moist grass, it deposited six young shells, each having 2–2½ whorls. The species is, it would seem, viviparous.

Helix Cooperi W. G. Binney Proc. Acad. N. S. Phila. 1858, p. 115.

Mr. Binney described this from specimens found by Dr. F. V. Hayden (Yellow Stone River Expl. Exped.), among the Black Hills of Nebraska. We can refer only to this a number of shells collected by Dr. Cooper on the east side of Mullan's Pass, in the Rocky Mountains, W. T., Lat. 46° 30′ N., at an elevation of 5500 feet.

The shells, however, attain a very much larger size than those described by Mr. Binney,—his (5 whorls) are diam. maj. 15, min. 13, alt. 9 mill., whereas Dr. Cooper's specimens (6 whorls) measure diam. maj. 25, min. 23, alt. 12 mill. In those before us the outer whorl is little deflected at the aperture, and the shell, altogether larger, is less globose ; the color is also different, Dr. Cooper's examples are generally of a light ash-grey color, the upper part prettily tesselated with reddish brown patches of varied shades, and the last whorl has two bands of the same color, one above and the other below the periphery. The surface in fresh specimens has a granulated appearance, the incremental striæ being crossed by numerous distinct impressed spiral lines.

This species has marked affinities with *H. strigosa* Gould, indeed, on a cursory examination might perhaps pass as a variety, but the difference in color and sculpturing, its more elevated spire, and narrower umbilicus, seem to entitle it to specific distinction.

We find a *colorless worn* specimen, with umbilicus more like that of *H. strigosa*, and which may be an elevated form of that species, or a variety of *H. Cooperi.*

This species also occurs on the Big Horn Mountains, Nebraska ; on the west side of the Wind River Mountains ; and on the Rio Piedra, W. New Mexico.

Helix solitaria Say Jour. Acad. N. S. Phila. ii., p. 157.

Dr. Cooper collected many specimens on both slopes of the Coeur d'Alêne Mountains, particularly in the bush and fern covered openings in the forests, at elevations exceeding 2500 feet. This well known species inhabits a wide area. Say described a single dead example from Lower Missouri. It occurs also in Michigan, Indiana, and Ohio. A small variety, sometimes without bands, is found on Strontian Island, Lake Erie. One of Dr. Cooper's specimens has a very unusual arrangement of color,—the entire shell is dark reddish brown, with a single pale band at the periphery.

The shell found by Dr. Hayden at Bridger's Pass, Nebraska, and referred to by Mr. W. G. Binney (Proc. Acad. N. S. Phila. 1858, p. 115) as a small variety of *H. solitaria* is evidently the young state of *H. Cooperi* W. G. Binney.

Helix arborea Say Nich. Enc. iv., pl. 4, f. 4.

Dr. Cooper met with this species in damp bottom lands along the lower valley of the Hell Gate River, at an elevation of about 4500 feet. The wide distribution of *H. arborea* is remarkable, it is found from Labrador to Texas, from Florida to Nebraska, also on the Rio Chama in New Mexico. It is likewise said by Bean to inhabit the island of Guadeloupe, West Indies. Férussac, in a letter to Say (1820), the original of which is in the possession of T. Bland, expresses his belief that *H. arborea* is found in Guadeloupe.

Helix striatella Anthony Jl. Bost. Soc. N. H. iii., pl. 3, f. 2.

Dr. Cooper also found this in the same locality as *H. arborea* Say. Its range is from Canada East to Kansas, and from Pembina on the Red River of the North to Virginia.

Succinea rusticana Gould Proc. Bost. Soc. N. H. 1846, p. 187.

This species was brought by the U. S. Exploring Expedition from Oregon. Dr. Cooper collected it on the Rocky Mountains of the Bitter Root Valley, at elevations from 2500 to 4500 feet.

The following fresh water species, as determined with the assistance of Messrs. Lea, Binney, and Prime, were also collected in the mountains by Dr. Cooper:

Melania plicifera Lea ⎫
Limnæa fragilis L. ⎪
———— humilis Say ⎪
Physa hypnorum L. ⎬ Hell Gate River.
———— heterostropha Say ⎪
Planorbis trivolvis Say ⎪
———— parvus Say ? ⎪
Sphærium occidentale Prime ⎭

Limnæa fragilis L. ⎫
———— bulimoides L. ⎪
———— desidiosa S. ⎬ Missouri River above the Falls.
Physa heterostropha S. ⎪
Sphærium striatinum Lam ⎭

Leptoxis.
Amnicola.
Ancylus.
Unio luteolus Lam.
Margaritana margaritifera L.

This latter was found in the " Missouri River above the Falls, and also in the Spokan River below Lake Coeur d'Alêne." It is the purple variety, hitherto only brought from the Pacific coast.